Queen of the City 2

The Life of a Female Rapper

An Urban Hood Romance

Tamicka Higgins

© 2015

Disclaimer

This is a work of fiction. Names, places, characters and events are all fictitious for the reader's pleasure. Any similarities to real people, places, events, living or dead are all coincidental.

This book contains sexually explicit content that is intended for ADULTS ONLY (+18).

Introduction

Big Tuck glared down the barrel of a 9 millimeter with a silencer on the tip of it. Lyric held the pistol in her hand, still naked and her heart set on revenge that wouldn't be satisfied until Big Tuck was dead. Images of Junie flashed in and out of her mind as Big Tuck sat on his bed, his stomach protruding and his chest dropping down because of his corpulence. He wasn't intimidated, not in the slightest. He had been in this position many times before, and he wasn't afraid to meet death.

"Bitch, are you fucking crazy? You will be dead before you walk out this room."

"You remember Junie?" I said, aiming the gun directly at him. He laughed to himself as he turned to place his feet on the ground.

"Who the fuck is Junie?"

"Muthafucka don't play dumb! You had him killed almost a year ago."

He put his hand on his forehead, "Bitch, do you know how many people I kill every year? How the fuck am I supposed to remember based on that?" He stood up, but I squeezed the trigger on the silenced weapon, sending one bullet flying past him into the mattress.

"Sit yo' fat ass back down, nigga or the next one is going through your head."

He put his hands up and sat back down on the bed, "Look bitch, I don't know no fucking Junie, and if I killed him, it was for good reason. Shit. Anybody I kill is for a good cause." He reached towards the nightstand as I fired another bullet into the pillow right next to him, "Bitch, I'm just getting a cigarette." He pulled it out of the drawer and lit the end of it, inhaling and blowing the smoke out slowly before saying,

"Look, if I did kill him, he deserved it. Tuck don't kill anybody that didn't deserve it."

"Fuck that shit—"

"Oh, wait," He said, cutting me off,

"I remember Junie. Hell yeah, tall, pretty ass muthafucka' with the dimples? Hell yeah. He was short on some money he owed me. I gave him ample time to pay me back but the nigga just… drug his feet. He tried to hoe me. You know." He blew smoke out of his mouth and said,

"I can't let a pussy ass nigga like that hoe Big Tuck. This my city and I guarantee, if you kill me, you'll—"

Pow! The cigarette fell from his hand as he slowly tumbled over onto the floor, making a small thud. I shot him right in his forehead and the blood poured from his dome, forming a small puddle around him. My top lip curled up as I stood in front of his dead body, naked and empowered. I felt like the chapter of my life with Junie could officially close as Big Tuck laid there, blood pouring out his body with his eyes wide open. I hurried and got dressed, keeping the gun close to me as if Big Tuck was going to get up from his gunshot wound and pull out another pistol. It was well past 15 minutes by the time I got to the door. As soon as I cracked it open, I was staring down the pipe of a double barrel shotgun. I dropped my pistol when the round was loaded into the barrel. Nas stood, holding the other end, "Where that nigga at, Lyric?" he said, moving past me and into the hotel room. I grabbed his arm and said,

"He's done, Nas. Come on, let's go!"

"The fuck you mean he's done?"

"I killed him. Let's fucking go!"

He walked in any way with his shotgun drawn, ready to squeeze the trigger. Keyonna was still knocked unconscious, sloped against the dresser. Big Tuck was laid out on the floor in his puddle of blood as dead as he was when I fired the shot. Nas looked over at me,

"You did this shit?"

"I told you I did. Now let's go, Nas! Come on!"

He yanked away from me, focusing on Keyonna. She was still breathing, so he put the barrel to her head. I pulled him back away from her, "Fuck her, Nas! Damn! You pull that fucking trigger, and no way we are getting out this Muthafuckin' building! She isn't shit! Come on!" He relaxed his grip on the shotgun, and we left the room. Outside in the hall, the bodies of his guards laid across the floor while Man-Man stood at the elevator waiting for us to get in. Nas grabbed my arm, and we walked past the bodies, one of them was still twitching just waiting for death to take completely over. Nas tucked the shotgun in his sleeve, and Man-Man concealed his in his waistband as we got off the elevator and headed for the back door of the hotel. It was early in the morning, so the activity in the hotel was at a minimum. Just like that, it was all over. We were gone, Big Tuck was dead, and I could finally lay Junie to rest inside my heart.

"You should've let me kill that bitch, Lyric."

"Nah, she straight."

"Fuck. How you know she ain't gon bring this shit back on us?"

"Because, she ain't like that. She ain't no snitch."

"Aight. Shit, if she pops back up, it's on you, though, Lyric."

"Aight. It's on me then."

He peered at me for a few moments before he leaned in and kissed me on the lips, "I can't believe you popped that nigga, though, you know what I'm saying? Shit. I didn't know you had it in you," he turned to look at Loc, "I came in the room, and that nigga was face down in his blood and shit. Gunshot straight through his fucking dome. My bitch is a killer, yall." It felt good hearing him speak that way about the stuff I did. As far as he knew, I did it for him, and I could let him live with that. Deep down inside, I knew who it was for, though, and I would have done it again without hesitation if I had to. I leaned my head back on the headrest and ran my hand across my belly. The issue with my pregnancy became more and more real every day. As the streetlights passed over us, nervousness slowly crept over me like a thief in the night. Here I was with a crazy ass boyfriend who was so ecstatic about having a baby that if he found out it wasn't his, I would have a hard time trying to explain myself while trying to keep us together. I didn't think he would kill me, but then again, I wouldn't put anything past him. He was ruthless as fuck whenever he got in those zones, so all I could do was hope and pray this seed was his. He put his hand on top of mine, coasting back and forth over my stomach.

"Maybe you should just chill for the next few months, Mama. I mean, shit. You can't be out here rapping and shit with my Lil' boy in yo' stomach. He gon' fuck around and come out retarded and I'ma be pissed."

I laughed, "First of all, how the fuck you know it's a boy?"

"Because, the first time I nutted in you, I was fucking you from the back. That's an automatic boy every time."

"Shit, how you know?"

He smiled the way Junie did whenever he was about to say some off the wall shit,

"Urban legend."

"Urban Legend my ass. It could be a girl."

"Yeah, it could be. If it is, we sending her ass back for a refund."

"Get the fuck off me, Nas."

He laughed, "I'm playing, Baby, I'm playing. If it's a girl, I'ma love her the same, you know that. I was just fucking with you." He put his arm around me as I cuddled up closer to him, silently pleading with God to make sure this baby belonged to Nas.

Chapter 1

"Push!"

"Aahhhhhhhhhh,"

I yelled as Nas stood next to me, anxiously holding my hand in the hospital room. The nurses were coaching me every step of the way as I did my best to push the baby out of me.

"Aight, honey. Just push again, aight."

"Fuck you, Nas! Fuck you! You're the reason I'm in this position! Get the fuck away from me!"

I yanked myself loose from his grasp as the doctor sat on a stool at the end of my bed with a bright ass light shining down between the middle of my legs. "Alright, Lyric. We're going to need you to give us another push, ok? Can you do that?"

I yelled out as if I was possessed, "Yes! Just, get this Lil muthafucka' out of me!"

"Alright, alright, Lyric. He's coming. Go ahead and push."

"Aaaaaaaaahhhhhhhhhh!"

They gave me an epidural, but I still felt brief spurts of pain that pierced through my body and made me feel as if I was about to pass out and die. I'd been shot before; those brief moments of pain were more excruciating than any gunshot wound. As soon as I heard him crying, though, it was like all the pain and discomfort I felt was gone. My anger turned to joy instantly as they carried him over to a table to clean him off. I looked over at Nas as he stood there, his eyes wide open, watching the life he believed he created to take its first breaths. I could tell he was fighting back tears, and it would have been a beautiful thing to have seen him cry. After they finished cleaning the baby off, one of the assistants looked towards Nas and said,

"Dad, you want to hold him?"

He didn't say anything, he just walked over to the table and held his arms out as they placed him gently in his grasp. He smiled, leaning in to kiss him on his face, walking carefully over to me so I could see him.

"Look, Mama, this is what we made."

He had a head full of hair and a wrinkled, old-looking face. His eyes moved around the room as we spoke like he was trying to figure out where the voices were coming from. Their color looked to be gray but the pamphlets I read also stated that their eyes were known to change colors for the first few months, so I tried not to fall in love with them. But him? I couldn't help but to instantly fall in love with my baby boy as soon as I saw him. The doctor walked up to Nas,

"Ok, Dad. Let's let Mom hold him close to her body—"

I cut him off, "So I can use my body heat to help regulate his."

The doctor smiled, "Exactly right. You talk like you've done this before."

"No, I just read a lot before I had him."

Nas placed him in my arms as I held his naked body tight against mine. It was incredible, finally holding the life that I held and talked to so often these past nine months. To think that two human beings are powerful enough to create another life whenever they come together sexually is an amazing thing to wrap your mind around.

"Hey, Mama's baby. Hey, sweetheart. You're the one that was giving me heartburn, making me throw up, and have all types of weird ass cravings. I should be giving you your first whooping right now, little boy."

His mouth moved in a smile as soon as I said that and that is when I knew, without a doubt, that this baby belonged to Nas. A slight dimple, smaller than the tip of my pinky finger, pushed his cheek in as he laid in my arms. I wiped a tear of relief from my eye; The relief that I didn't have to worry about Nas leaving me because of a misunderstanding. I reached down and kissed him on his forehead as Nas put his arm around me and kissed me on the cheek.

"Nas, did you come up with a name for him? Is he going to be Nas, Jr?"

"Nah. I don't want him to be a junior."

I looked at him quizzically, "What? Why not?"

"Because, since I am a king, he will be the prince. Prince Nasir Jones."

From that point on, our son was known as Prince Nasir Jones and it was the perfect name of a child born to a king and queen. Since I murdered Big Tuck a half year ago, Nas moved right into his place as the kingpin of the city. He had cocaine and weed flooding the streets of Milwaukee, picking up territory on every side of town. Anybody that opposed him usually ended up dead, and he wasn't afraid to do it at any time of day. He even had some local police and law officials on his payroll to help keep his business thriving. All of that was going on while I sat on top of the city with him, helping him run his business flawlessly. I was like the eyes that watched his back at all times and kept shit in line when he was too busy fucking around with dumb shit to see it himself. The king is the most important piece in the game but the queen was the most powerful piece without a doubt, and we both understood and respected that. We stayed in our lanes and kept the respect between us. He appreciated my blunt honesty and how I never backed down from him and I appreciated how he handled shit fearlessly whenever it came up. He didn't bat an eye when dangerous situations came up but more importantly, he made sure I was safe whenever it did. The only thing he kept a close watch on more than his drugs and his money was me. Two things women want in relationships are security and to feel protected. Nas provided both of those things for me flawlessly. He was a tougher, stronger version of Junie and as much as I thought that killing Big Tuck would allow me to put the thoughts I had of Junie to rest, it never did. Junie was alive, and now he was alive even more because of Prince. To me, he looked more like Junie than Nas and that, in itself, freaked me out.

After a few days, the doctors gave us the green light to leave the hospital and head home. Nas moved us out to the suburbs, away from all the drama that was going on in the city. He dropped $300,000 on a house for us out in Wauwatosa, a suburb of Milwaukee. Out there, the police showed up twice as fast as the noise was little to none. He figured it would be safer for us out there than anywhere else in the city. He even paid the mortgage off on Big Mama's house so Uncle Stew and Vinny wouldn't have to worry about paying it anymore. He figured it was the least he could do since he was taking me away from them but he said he just wanted me safe. I wasn't feeling it too much though because I was a city girl and I was used to the busyness of it all, but all that shit had to change when Prince was born. It was no longer about what I wanted to do but what was best for him. Loc stayed out there with us for added protection. It seemed like he never slept, though. Like that muthafucka was a robot or something.

We pulled up to our house in the middle of the block. It was a large, four-bedroom home with a big ass front yard that we paid some Mexicans to come by and keep clean every month.

"I got him, mama. You are just gon' head in the house and chill."

I smiled and let him bring in Prince. I knew he wasn't going to be around much, but whenever he was, I could tell he was going to spoil me and want me to calm down. It's one of the things I loved about him. As hard as he was with other people, and trust me, that nigga was hard a fuck, he was just the opposite with me. He brought Prince in and sat him on the couch in his car seat. He was fast asleep.

"Aight Ma, I gotta run to the house and check up on shit. I haven't been there all day."

"Aight baby."

"Shit, hit me if you need anything. Loc will be here. Send that nigga out if you need something from the store. I just want you to stay here and take care of our Prince."

"Aight, I got it."

He leaned in to kiss me, but I held on to his arm.

"Whassup, Ma?"

I whispered into his ear,

"I wanna fuck."

"Didn't the doctor say we had to wait for that shit? I mean, I don't want to start fuckin', and then you start bleedin' all over the place and shit. I think I'd fuckin' pass out."

"Nigga, all the blood and shit you've seen, and you gon pass out over that?"

"Ma, that's an entirely different scenario, you know what I'm sayin'? A fuckin' pussy leakin' blood is different from a nigga leakin' blood. That shit is completely different."

I laughed, "You right. Well, what if I...."

I reached over and unbuckled his pants. His dick fell out of his boxers as soon as I tugged on them a little bit. I was horny as fuck. I hadn't had sex for almost a month, and the fuckin' doctors had the nerve to tell me that I couldn't fuck for a few more months? I needed some dick to pacify me. I pulled it out and put my mouth around it, sucking it slowly until he got rock hard. He put his hand on my head as I went back and forth, licking his dick from the bottom up and sucking on the tip. He grabbed the sides of my face, guiding me back and forth as my lips gripped his dick. He pushed my head all the way down until it was deep in my throat and then let me back up. I looked him directly in his eyes, and he grabbed my head and pushed me all the way down on it again. My pussy got wetter just by the way he took control, pushing all of his dick inside my mouth and fuckin' with Keyonna got me used to taking in a big cock like this. He came in a matter of minutes and as long as he was satisfied, so was I.

"That's why you are my bitch," He said, pulling his pants back up, "I'ma be through here later on. Aight?"

I wiped my mouth and said, "Aight, Nas." I went to the bathroom and cleaned myself up. Prince was still asleep when I was finished, and I was in a big ass house with damn near nothing to do.

A few months had passed, and Prince was one of the easiest babies I'd ever been around. He only cried when he was hungry or needed to be changed, and he slept all night when he hit two months. Nas went back and forth between our home and the drug houses, but he only stayed a few days at a time here. I wished he could have stayed more, but I understood the game. He had a business to run, and I was cool with it, but I was tired as shit of stayin' in the house. I convinced him to let me get a babysitter for Prince. He wasn't feeling it at first, but I told him I wasn't a fucking stay-at-home mother, and I wasn't meant to be one. I'd already been cooped up in the house with Prince for over two months, and the shit was making me stir crazy.

"Damn, Lyric. Why can't you just stay yo' ass in the fuckin' house?"

"Fuck that shit, Nas. When you met me, you knew I was doing my thang fuckin' rappin' and shit. You can't expect me just to be cool with stayin' in this fuckin' house with Prince."

"Well, shit changes when you have a baby."

I paused, "Well, then you stay yo' ass in this house with him and let me run shit. You know I can."

He laughed, "Let you run it?"

I walked over to him and looked him squarely in the eyes. He was a few inches taller than me, but I didn't care, he knew I wasn't backing down from anybody,

"Yeah, let me run it. I know how to make sure that shit stays in line. Them bitches know not to fuck with me, and the niggas know I will pull out on them just as quick as you will."

"Yeah, aight. We'll see."

"So, I'ma get a babysitter so I can start movin' around and shit."

He grabbed me around my waist, "Look Ma, I just don't want shit to happen to you or Prince. Shit, I got a girl and a baby boy now, so muthafuckas know I got a weakness. The more people you love, the weaker you are, you feel me? They get to y'all; they get to me." I placed my hands on the sides of his face, "They not gon' get to me and if they do, they gon have a fuckin' problem on their hands. Trust me, aight? Yo' bitch know how to handle herself." He took a deep breath and finally gave in to me,

"You know somebody who will take care of Prince?"

I looked over at Prince as he lay asleep on our bed. Everything he had on was Jordan Brand but what did you expect from a baby of two drug dealers? The Jordan symbol was like the sign that represented the dope game for ballers, "I know somebody who would be perfect for watching him." His hands slid down to my ass, gripping a handful of it as he looked behind me into the mirror. I turned around and saw his smile, and that was the only hint I needed.

We went downstairs to the front room, and he fucked me right in front of the living room window. The curtains were pulled back for anybody to walk or drive past and see us. I wouldn't have been surprised if the neighbors across the street stopped to look outside their window and catch us in action. He bent me over the back of the couch and smacked my ass while he went in from behind, pulling my hair and slapping my behind. He fucked me in a way that showed that he was releasing pent-up aggression from months of not fucking. It also helped me believe that he wasn't fucking around on me because I don't think any nigga would have this kind of energy if he were fucking other chicks. I arched my back so I could feel his dick deeper inside me. I could see the shadow of my titties swinging back and forth in the mirror as a few cars drove past, oblivious to what was going on inside our house. The thrill of somebody catching us made my pussy drip even more. I thought back to the time we fucked down by the lake at the art exhibit. That rush I felt then crept back into me as I looked in the window, catching a glimpse of his face. My mind slipped into a fantasy world where Junie replaced Nas, and his long strokes slowed down. "No, speed up," I murmured as the hard pounding came back. Shortly, I snapped out of the fantasy as Nas pulled out and came on my ass. I moaned as I felt his warm cum drip on me. I turned as he stood in front of me, his muscular chest was completely tatted. I looked a little closer, noticing some new ink he had on the right side of his chest. In the spot that represented his heart, it was like that portion of his chest was ripped off, and inside it read, *Lyric & Prince*. It was simple, but it was heartfelt. I stood up and kissed him on his lips.

"I gotta go, Baby."

"I know, I know."

"Make sure you let me know when you drop him off at the sitter. Let me know the address and all that shit in case I need to come through there for any reason."

"Aight, Daddy."

He spent a few minutes in the bathroom and with that, he was gone. I heard Prince crying upstairs a few moments later. I knew exactly where to take him, but I had to make a quick stop first.

I hadn't visited the cemetery since I'd been out the hospital. It had been too breezy for me to take Prince out there, so I had to wait until the weather broke a little bit. I carried Prince in my arms with a bouquet of flowers in my other hand. Her gravestone was huge. Nas had her body exhumed and reburied with a bigger headstone next to her.

The way he cared for Big Mama after she died made me believe that he would have done even more for her if he knew her. Every time I spoke to him about her, I said nothing but good things that made him regret not having the chance to know her. He felt like doing these type of things was the next best thing to do because she deserved to be remembered in the best way possible. As soon as we walked to her grave, Prince smiled and made those cute baby noises he seemed to be so fond of making. His dimple had gotten a little bigger since birth, but his eyes were still gray, the same color of Big Mamas. I'd hoped that they wouldn't change.

"Hey, Big Mama. I miss you so much, I do. It's just not the same without you here. I don't have anybody to threaten my life for not doing something or to get on me when I'm out of line. I think that, because of that, I've gotten a little out of control. I know you see me up there, and you know what I'm doing, but all I can say is I don't know what else to do. hadn't found that faith that you had so much of when you were down here,"

Prince yelled as if to get my attention,

"Oh, and this is Prince. Sitting here talking to you, I forgot I was even holding your great-grandson," I wiped a tear from my eye. "I think you two will have the same eye color. At least I'm hoping his won't change. It will help me feel like you're with me even more than you are now. I know you can't hold him, and it's probably making you sad that you can't, but there will be a time when you'll be able to, I'm sure of it. I haven't checked on Uncle Stew and Vinny in a while, you know, since Nas moved us out to Wauwatosa but I'm going to do better with that. I talk to Vinny though, and he says Uncle Stew is still staying out of trouble, but I'm going over there as soon as I leave here. Listen to me, Big Mama; I love you a lot. A whole lot and I'ma do everything I can down here to make you proud of me, ok? I miss you, and I can't wait to see you again."

I turned to walk away, my eyes blurry from the tears that kept falling when I was talking to her. I felt her presence surrounding me while I was there. A comforting feeling that let me know that she heard me and she will always be there for me. The only problem was that I couldn't see her and now that I think about it, it's the same issue I had with God. Maybe now, it would change for the better.

I pulled up to Big Mama's house. Vinny's car was parked in the garage when I showed up. The front door was open to let the breeze blow through the screen door. The grass was cut, and the bushes were trimmed. They were doing a good job at keeping Big Mama's house up. Just then, Uncle Stew stepped from the side of the house with sheers in his hand.

"Lyric! How you been! Is that Prince you got with you?" he asked, walking up to me as he took his gloves off. His hair was trimmed just like the bushes on the side of the house and for once, he looked as if he would be able to go out and bag a couple of women. I didn't realize how handsome he was until now, "Yeah, this Prince." He walked over to me as he wiped the sweat from his brow.

"I would hold him but I been out here in this yard and I don't want to have him smellin' like the outside."

He bent down and kissed him on his forehead.

"Hey little fella," Prince cooed, "Man, you lookin' just like yo' mama. And you got yo' Big Mama's eyes. Look at there," he said with a broad smile on his face.

"Is Vinny in there?"

"Yeah, he should be. He was off today and he just been sittin' in there playing video games. I told that boy to come out here and help me in the yard, but all he says is, *yeah, I'll be there. I got one more quarter left* and then that boy never shows up. Lazy rascal!"

I laughed, "Yeah, that sound just like Vinny."

We went into the house, and Vinny had his leg up on the table playing his Playstation 4 on the living room TV. They had upgraded a lot of stuff since they no longer had a mortgage to pay. New furniture, new TV's, and they even had the house repainted. I was proud of what they were doing to Big Mama's house. Vinny smiled and put his controller down.

"Oh, Shit! What up, Prince!" he said, walking over to grab him out of my arms.

"Oh, nigga, Prince the only one you see?"

"My bad, my bad. What up L," he said as he kept his eyes on Prince, "Man, this little nigga gettin' big! What you feedin' him? Shit."

"The Similac."

Uncle Stew spoke up,

"Lyric, you know if Mama were still here, she would have a fit with you feeding that baby that similac."

He was right. I could hear her now, "Girl, yo' titties didn't get that big just for somebody else's pleasure! They got that big because The Good Lord knew that yo' breastmilk would be the best type of milk for that little boy! Now, do what you was supposed to do with that milk and let that boy suck on yo' titty!" She was just blunt like that, but I tried it a few times, and it was just too painful. Like I said when I went to the cemetery, she's not here to keep me in line and just by looking at how I was when she was here versus now, it would be easy to tell.

"I know Unc, but hey, he's still healthy, so that's all that matters to me right now."

Vinny glanced at me,

"So, when yo' ass about to get back out there and start rappin' again? You know niggas is just waitin' for you to pop up again."

"I know. Shit, I ain't had the time really because I was in the crib with Prince all day but that shit finally change. I got him a sitter."

"Word? Who?"

"I don't know for sure yet, but if it's cool, I'll let you know who it is."

"Well, shit, who you got in mind then?"

I glanced over at Prince as he lay on the couch, flapping his arms like a fish out of water. His dimple pushed his cheek in as he smiled. *Damn, he looks just like Junie*, I said to myself, smiling back at Prince. I knew exactly where I was going to take him, and I had a feeling that they wouldn't hesitate to take him in for a few hours every day either. I had no doubt in my mind that they would take him in with open arms. Prince cooed again as if he could read my thoughts. He was going with his grandparents.

Chapter 2

I showed up at their home unannounced. I figured it would be a pleasant surprise because they hadn't seen me since they showed me baby pictures of Junie and Nas together. Serena, Junie's older sister, came to the door. Her smile became stale as she looked down towards the baby seat I was carrying.

"Hey Lyric, umm... who's baby is that?"

"It's mine."

Her smile completely faded away at that point as she stood at the door, almost hesitant to let me in. The look on her face told me she was confused and almost heartbroken that I showed up here with a baby. Almost to say, *How dare you come here?*.

"Can I come in? He's heavy."

"No. You can't."

I sat Prince's car seat down on the patio and lowered my eyes, looking directly at her. She was still away at college the time I came over and her parents showed me pictures of Junie and his little brother. Moments later, Mrs. Butler came to the door, "Hey, Lyric!" she said as her eyes dropped down to the baby seat. Her smile never left her face, "Oh, my! And who do we have here?" she said, bending down to get a better view of him. Her smile froze, the same way Serena's did. She slowly shifted her sight back towards me, covering her mouth. She knew it right away as she picked up the baby seat, "Come... Come on in, Lyric. Please." I grabbed the baby bag and walked past Serena as she stood in the doorway, completely confused as to what was going on.

"Allen, honey? Um, can you come here, please? Like, right now," Mrs. Butler said as she sat Prince's car seat down on the couch. She kept her hand over her mouth, shaking her head slowly like she was looking at something that was completely unfeasible. Allen walked into the room; his eyes lit up when he saw me, "Lyric! Hey, sweetheart! How have you been?" He reached over to embrace me as he heard Prince giggle just to his right. He turned towards him, saying the same thing his wife said when he was out on the patio. Stacey grabbed his arm, "No, baby. Look at him. Just look." He bent down to get a better view of Prince, and it was as if his heart dropped. He looked back towards me, then towards his wife. "Oh my goodness," he said as he looked back in my direction, "May I hold him?"

"Of course."

He picked him up, Prince's gray eyes still maintaining their color. His dimple was now clearly seen as he smiled in his grandfather's arms. He kissed him on his cheek and then passed him to Stacey as tears rolled down her cheeks. "He is gorgeous," she said as he sat comfortably in her arms. Serena watched what was going on, trying to put things together herself. She finally spoke up when she couldn't figure it out,

"Uh, Mom? Dad? Somebody want to tell me what is going on here?"

I spoke up, "I will."

We all sat down in the front room, and I began,

"A little over a half year after Junie died, I met a guy named Nas. I mean, he looked just like Junie at times, and it scared me. I just thought I wasn't over him, you know? So I didn't pay much attention to it, but his mannerisms, the things he said, his smile, and his dimples—I mean everything he did reminded me of Junie. Well, one day me and Nas were at the mall and I run into Mrs. Butler—"

She interrupted me as she held Prince in her arms,

"Baby, just call me Mom, ok?"

It was a little weird to me to call her that, but I just did it. After all, she was like a mother figure to me when me and Junie were together.

"Ok. I was with Nas at Mayfair, and then we ran into... Mom... and she was looking at Nas like he was familiar. Then she asked me to come by here so she could talk to me about something. I showed up, and then they pull out these pictures of Junie when he was younger."

Allen got up to get the photo album, buried at the bottom of the drawer so nobody could see it. He pulled out pictures of Junie when he was younger, and the resemblance he had with Prince was uncanny. He passed some of the pictures to me and the others to Serena as we both looked through them, glancing up at Prince now and then to compare.

"Serena, this little boy is your nephew."

There was an uncomfortable pause as she switched between the pictures and Prince. She had her mouth hung open, ready to say something but it seemed as if no words could escape her mouth. I didn't know how much of the story she knew at this point or if she knew anything at all. She let the pictures fall out of her hand and stood up.

"Wait a minute. So, y'all are telling me that I have another little brother out here somewhere. And not only that, but he somehow connected with Lyric, and they had a baby, and now the baby looks just like Junie?"

As I heard her speak, I realized myself how crazy it came off. Stacey remained on the couch, hugging and squeezing Prince as he laughed and welcomed her touch. Allen stood up and walked over to Serena, throwing his arms around her as her eyes bubbled with tears. She moved his arms away from her after just a few moments,

"No, no Daddy! Y'all," she wiped her eyes, "Y'all can't just tell me all this right now! Y'all can't! It's too much! I'm 28 years old, and I'm just now hearing that I have another little brother!? And on top of that, he had a baby with Lyric and…"

She stopped speaking for a moment doing her best to collect herself, then she continued,

"What happened? How do I have a little brother that I don't even know about!?"

"Sweetheart, it was just a lot going on at the time. I'm surprised you don't remember seeing him around, but you were just turning four when all of this happened. It…" Stacey paused, trying to collect herself, "It was just a bad situation. If we could do it over, we would have just done our best to make it work, but we panicked. We were already young, we had two children, and we were on the verge of being evicted. Our car was repossessed, I mean, it was just a terrible situation to try to bring another baby in to. We did what we thought was best for the family. We just couldn't care for everyone at that time."

She stood up and handed Prince to me as she went over to Serena and hugged her tight. Allen followed in right behind her as all three of them held each other, crying from past mistakes and whole lives that they missed out on. I saw, first hand, what the pain would have been if I gave Prince up for adoption or even worse, went through with the abortion. I glanced at him as he smiled in my arms, reaching towards my face. I kissed his hands and hugged him tight as Stacey called out to me,

"Lyric, come on over here with my grandbaby. You two are officially a part of this family now."

I walked over to their huddle as they embraced me like I was one of their children. I could feel the love radiated between all four of us, and it was something I hadn't felt since before Big Mama got sick. I appreciated it more than they would ever know. Serena wiped her eyes,

"I'm sorry about earlier when you came to the door, Lyric. I just didn't expect you to—"

I cut her off, "I know, girl. Trust me, I know, and I understand. You were just protective of Junie. You don't have to apologize."

"Can I hold him?"

I passed Prince to Serena as she kissed him right on his dimple. It seemed to be love at first sight as she held him the same way Stacey did when she picked him up.

"Oh my God, he does look like Junie. With the little dimple and everything and oh my goodness, his eyes! He is going to be a heartbreaker."

"I don't even wanna think that far down the line," I said, smiling.

"Can I meet my other brother?"

I thought about Nas's reaction when I told him about Stacey and Allen. He was adamant about not wanting to see them or have anything to do with them. From what I could sense, he had some bitterness in his heart about his parent's giving him up for adoption. That was the one thing I was worried about when bringing Prince over here; I knew they would want to meet Nas.

"Yeah, I mean, he's real busy and everything with work."

"What does he do?" Serena asked anxiously. "It's crazy to know that I have a brother out there that I know nothing about."

"He, um, he's a producer like Junie was."

Her mouth dropped, "You've got to be kidding me!"

"No, I'm not. I said the same thing myself. Junie and Nas were twins."

"Yeah," his father spoke up, "they were just about a year apart. Your mom and I got busy sooner than we were supposed after we had Tyrell and—"

"Uh, Dad?" Serena cut him off, "that's too much information. We didn't need to know all of that."

"Hey, it's a part of life! You wouldn't be here if it weren't for us getting busy back in—"

"Dad!"

He and Stacey laughed as we all sat back down. I brought up the idea of them babysitting Prince while I went out and ran errands during the day. She was completely fine with the notion, especially since she stayed home now. It didn't appear that Serena was in the business of having any babies anytime soon since she was a recent college graduate looking for work, and Prince was just another version of Junie as far as Stacey was concerned. We worked it out that she would have him Monday through Saturday in the afternoon and be on call for emergencies. Prince hadn't cried one time since we had been at his grandparents' house. That let me know, even more so, that bringing him here was the right thing to do. The only problem I saw in the future was what Nas would do if he found out that Prince's babysitter was his mother. That was something I didn't think I would be prepared to handle.

Chapter 3

"What the fuck did you think would happen? You thought nobody was coming to the stash house today? Huh? You thought shit was sweet, didn't you?"

"Come on, man. I'm sorry, I just needed a little extra, you know what I'm sayin'? Shit is kinda' tight for me right now."

"Kinda tight? Kinda tight, muthafucka? So, you take money from my own son's mouth for this shit? You take money from my family because it's tight for you? Word? That's how you roll, huh?"

He was on his knees, begging for leniency as tears fell out his eyes.

"Please, I just...I just lost my head for a second; that's it. I promise it won't happen again. I promise."

"Yeah, you're right. It won't happen again."

Pow! The bullet left the pistol and pierced him right on the side of his head. Blood splattered against the wall from the hole that appeared right in his temple. A few men stood behind me, watching the blood spill from his head as he lay on the ground convulsing just before his eyes rolled to the back of his skull. I put the gun back on my waist and turned around as the dope boys stood in front of me.

"Let that be a lesson, aight? All shit done in the darkness comes to the light. Make sure this nigga gets disposed of."

I walked out of the stash house, a vacant home right in the middle of the hood on Milwaukee's East Side. Slowly but surely, I was becoming respected throughout our drug operation. I was not just known as "Nas's Bitch," but I was known as "Lyric." Throughout it all, I learned the perfect balance between strength and weakness that a woman needs to have. I showed a bit of frailty whenever I was around Nas to help him understand that I needed him but when he wasn't around, the strength of who I was shined bright like stars at midnight. I'd love to think that I got it from my Mom. Uncle Stew would always tell me that I had her mentality, and he saw her in me every time I snapped about something. He said that he could see her fire inside of me, and I could only imagine what kind of things she did when she was my age before she got strung out. My phone rang when I stepped outside,

"How was the spot?"

"Jordan's ass got caught with his hand in the cookie jar."

"No shit?"

"No shit."

"You handle it?"

"Yeah, it's taken care of."

"No doubt. Good shit, Ma. They need to make sure they see an example of what happens in case anybody else got the urge to get sticky fingers. If it was me, though, I'da brought him back to the crib and had fun with him."

"That's yo' thing, bae. I'm just about gettin' the shit done. No stalling."

"No doubt. I'll see you at the house later on."

"Aight."

I got in my car and left. I hadn't hit the rap scene at all since I started dropping Prince off at his grandparents' house. Vinny told me the streets was calling for me, but I didn't have the desire to go back out there in it. All my attention went to

Nas and what he had going on, and I was cool with it. Ever since Remy was murdered in broad daylight, I hadn't had anybody else step to me out of line like that. Nas put fear into everyone and made them think twice about fucking with me. Nas was the gentlest dude I had known but on the outside looking in, his temper was worse than Big Tucks. I literally couldn't count the number of people he killed or had maimed since I gave birth to Prince. Just like most kingpins, though, I knew his time on top would come to an end, but I just hoped that his end meant prison and not death. I couldn't handle another boyfriend being taken from me by the grave.

I had stopped at Big Mama's house before I went to pick Prince up from Mrs. Butler's. Vinny's car was gone, but I didn't know if Uncle Stew was around or not. I still had a key to the house, so either way, it wouldn't have been a problem. I opened the door.

"Unc? You in here?"

Silence flooded through the house as I closed the door behind me. Everything was clean, the floors were mopped and vacuumed, and the dinnerware that sat on top of the dining room table was dusted clean. The dishes in the kitchen were washed and put away. If I didn't know any better, I would have believed that big mama came down from heaven and did it herself. I walked into her room, and everything was still the way I left it when I cleaned her room up right before she died. I could feel the peace in there as soon as I passed beneath her doorframe. *Big Mama*, I said to myself, *I wish you were here*. I kicked off my shoes and lay on her bed, removing the pistol that was on my waist and placing a few small bags of coke under the bed. I forgot I put the little baggies in my pocket when I took them from Jordan, right before I murdered him for thieving. Next thing I knew, I was sound asleep.

I woke up to the smell of eggs and bacon cooking in the kitchen. My watch read 6:49 pm, so I wondered who was out there cooking breakfast so late. As I crept closer to the kitchen, I heard singing. I couldn't make out the name of the song, but I'd heard Big Mama sing the same one sometimes. I walked into the kitchen, rubbing my finger across my eyes to get a better view of the person scrambling eggs and flipping bacon over on the stove. My mama stood with an apron on; her hair tied back in a ponytail and a big smile on her face when she looked over to see me standing there,

"Hey, Lyric! I know it's late but I just had a taste for some bacon, eggs, and sausage right now. Come on, grab a plate. I made enough for both of us."

I looked around, hoping it wasn't a dream. For as long as I could remember, I always fantasized about having moments like this with my mother just to pick her brain and see how much of her was really in me. I walked over to the table and pulled out a chair as she scraped eggs onto my plate and said,

"Now, I didn't put that much salt on them. I got high blood pressure and that salt won't do anything good for me right now. You can sprinkle some on if you want, but it's hereditary, so chances are, you have it, but you don't know it. Have you gotten checked out yet?"

"Checked out for what?"

"For you blood pressure, girl! What did you think I was talking about?"

"I'm sorry, I was just—"

"You were just not payin' attention, that's all. It's ok."

She walked over and put four pieces of bacon on my plate.

"The bacon ain't good for my pressure either but who can turn down a plate of crispy bacon? I know I can't."

She fixed her plate and tossed the apron across the back of her chair and then sat down next to me at the table. I started to eat, but she smacked my hand causing me to drop the strip of bacon I held onto. She said,

"Have you lost your mind? We don't eat anything until we thank the Good Lord for blessing us with this meal."

I connected my hand with hers as she prayed with such power and strength that I was beginning to think she was Big Mama instead of my mama. From the pictures and everything I knew about her, she didn't seem like the type that would be conscious of God, let alone know how to pray like that. As she finished, we opened our eyes,

"Ok, child. Now you can eat but hurry up; Mama doesn't have a lot of time."

"Where do you have to go?"

She smiled as she sprinkled pepper onto her plate but she didn't respond. She took a bite of her eggs, patiently waiting for me to say something.

"Um…"

"Spit it out, girl. Like I say, I don't have much time, and I know you have a lot to ask."

"Who am I?"

She swallowed another bite of eggs,

"You are Lyric Sutton. My daughter."

"No, I mean. Who am I?"

"You are my daughter."

She kept eating her food as I realized that whatever this was in front of me was only sent to answer my questions exactly the way I asked them. I thought for a few moments as she took a bite of her bacon, still patiently waiting for me to ask her anything I could think of,

"Why am I the way I am?"

She took a napkin and wiped her mouth,

"Now that is a great question. You are living out every passion and desire I had when I was your age. I wanted to be a rapper, a queen pen and have a son that I could teach the game to. You were never created to play a subordinate role; you have been set up to rule. That was my desire when I was younger, a matter of fact, just a little older than you. But as I grew up into an older woman, I realized that everything I wanted was nothing. All of these things pass away and in the end, it leaves us with nothing but regrets. One of the most painful things to die with are regrets, and the other? Do you know what the other is?"

"No, ma'am."

"Unreached potential. There is a path that you can take, and you will be left with neither one to worry about. However, there is a way you can take that will leave you to die with both of them. What I can tell you since you are my daughter, is that you will undoubtedly pick the wrong path, but there will be redemption for you if you are sure to keep your eyes open for it. I guarantee you that you will find it if you look for it."

She took another bite of eggs and looked at her watch, "Oh, shoot! Now I gotta get going." As she stood up, I reached out to her, but my hand moved right through her arm. She looked back at me, her eyes beginning to water, "I'm sorry, baby. I wish I could stay, but your uncle is coming home. Matter of fact, he is in the room now, and I can't let him see me. He wouldn't know how to handle it." I reached out for her and suddenly, I felt her arm turn into flesh and bones, "Mama! Mama!" I yelled out, pulling on her arm.

When I came to, Uncle Stew was sitting on the edge of the bed, looking at me as if he had just seen a ghost. "Lyric, it's your uncle. Are you alright?" I jumped away from him as my mind slowly began to come back to reality. I peered around the room slowly as if to make sure I wasn't dreaming anymore. Uncle Stew sat on the bed just waiting for me to say something.

"Are you alright?"

I rubbed my eyes. "I'm good. I'm good, Unc," I said, sitting on the edge of the bed.

"How long have you been here?"

"I think for about an hour or so."

"Ok. You hungry?"

"No, I'm good."

"Alright. I'll leave you in here then. Let me know if you need anything."

He walked out of the room as I sat there, piecing together what just happened in my dream. *Mama was beautiful,* I thought to myself. She looked as if she was in her 50's but the thing is, I saw traces of myself inside of her without having to think hard at all. It was automatic. I glanced over at the picture of her that sat on Big Mama's desk. She wore a loose t-shirt with a cigarette hanging out her mouth, looking at the camera as if she was unprepared for the picture. I smiled and shook my head as I got up. I straightened out the bed and began to walk out of the door before I spun around. I forgot about the pistol I brought in with me. I grabbed it from under the bed and left. The time was coming for me to pick up Prince from his grandmother's house. Uncle Stew yelled out to me as I walked, like a zombie, through the front room,

"Lyric, you sure you're alright?"

"Yeah, I'm sure Unc. I'm sure."

"Well, alright, if you say so. I know Mama's room has the best sleep, but whenever I lay in there, I have some weird dreams myself. They are real, um…What's the word I'm looking for?" he said, snapping his fingers together to recollect. I helped him,

"Insightful?"

"Yeah, that's it. Real insightful."

"I see that now," I said as I opened the door.

"Love you, Lyric."

"Love you too, Unc."

I drove down to Mrs. Butler's house. Prince was making all kinds of baby noises as soon as I walked through the door. Stacey hugged me and Prince's eyes widened as he smiled, a line of slobber dripping down the side of his mouth.

"Hey, mama's baby," I said, picking him up into my arms.

"That boy is a joy, a complete joy!"

"I know, I missed my little man today."

I walked over and placed him in his car seat as Stacey prepared his baby bag. I could see that there was something on her mind, but I just didn't know what it was. It was the way she was solemnly placing the things in his bag and moving around the house as if she didn't want him to leave.

"Mom, what's wrong?"

She sighed, "No. No, it's not my place to say anything."

"What is it about?"

"Prince."

"Well, you're his grandmother, so you have more of a place than you think, so go ahead."

"I know that you're involved in some bad things, Lyric."

I glanced towards her with a look of surprise.

"What? What do you mean bad things?"

She placed a few more items in his bag, "Just. Some things that I don't believe Prince should be around. Now, I know you're a big girl, and you can handle yourself, but I just don't want anything to happen to my grandson."

"Listen, Mom? I don't know what bad things you think I'm involved in, but I'm not. Who is telling you this?"

"I have a friend over at the Milwaukee Police Department. She came by here the other day, and we were just talking, you know, and some things about you just casually came up."

"Just casually came up? I don't understand."

"She told me that a girl named Lyric and a man named Nas were being looked at for murder."

"Wait, what? Murder? Can she even talk to you about that kind of stuff?"

"She was mentioning it to me just to see if I knew anything about it, you know? I guess it would be the same thing as putting it on TV as a breaking news report."

I stood up and grabbed the baby seat before I asked,

"What did you tell them?"

"I didn't say anything, Lyric. Listen, I love you, and I don't want anything to happen to you, Prince, or my other son. I just..."

"You just what?"

"Never mind. Listen, I'll be here tomorrow, ok? Are you still going to bring Prince by?"

I paused for a minute as a million thoughts flooded in and out of my mind. I hid my nervousness as Stacey stood in front of me, desperately waiting for me to answer her. I saw the look of concern on her face and even though I was nervous about the situation, I didn't think she would be one to point the police in my direction.

"Yes, Mom. I'll bring him tomorrow."

"Ok."

She hugged me, and I was gone. On the way home, I called Nas and let him know to meet me at our house tonight. If we were being looked at for the murder, we both had to make sure each other were on the same page. I wasn't going to prison. Fuck that shit.

Chapter 4

Nas came home in a blur, nervous about what I told him. He paced back and forth in the living room as Prince looked at him smiling as if he was doing it for his entertainment.

"I covered all the tracks. The cameras, we went out the back and everything. I had that shit planned thorough, Ma. Ain't no way they on to us," he said, turning to me, "Who told you that? Who said they were lookin at us?" Prince started whining, so I picked him up out of his car seat, "I just heard some niggas talkin' when I was out." He peered at me, knowing the story wasn't making sense. "Lyric, I'm sayin', who, though?"

"The woman I take Prince to during the day. She said she had a cop friend that was passing the info to her to see if she knew anything."

"Oh my God, Lyric. Did she fuckin' say anything to her? Did that bitch say somethin'?" he said, approaching me with the killer rage that boiled in his eyes whenever he was about to react. His aggression made Prince flinch in my arms, and his eyes began to water. "Nigga, calm the fuck down, aight? You scarin' Prince." Nas looked over at Prince, causing his aggression to switch off.

He sat down next to us on the couch as be bent over and kissed Prince on the cheek. I could tell he was nervous, I mean, that went without saying, but kings don't react like this. Not the king I knew. He ran his hands over his face, knocking his fitted cap off his head and onto the floor.

"Look, Mrs. Butler didn't say anything, aight? I've been knowing her for a long time; you know what I'm saying? She wouldn't do that shit."

"How you know, Lyric?"

"What you mean? I just told you."

"Can I meet her?"

I paused. The irony of everything was coming full swing and with the state of mind he was in right now, I didn't want him to meet her. He was anxious to do anything to cover his tracks and even though I didn't think he would harm her, I definitely wouldn't put it past him. "Meet her for what?" I asked, Prince cooing in the background.

"I just want to see for myself; you know what I'm saying? I want to feel her out to see what she is on."

"You don't trust me?"

"Yeah but shit, if you say she ain't snitching, then what the fuck? Let me see for myself."

"Nah, cuz I know you on some bullshit right now. Mrs. Butler is good people, Nas. She ain't fuckin'—"

"Aye," he said, cutting me off, "I said I wanna meet the bitch so let me meet her. The fuck is wrong with you?"

I couldn't front, the way he snapped at me turned me on. I felt disrespected but at the same time, my pussy got wet just by him taking control like that. I glanced at Prince as he sat in my lap, looking back and forth between us. My mind put both of them in my view and for a moment, Junie sat across from me. I saw the worry in his eyes when he knew I was going to take Nas to meet his mother. Honestly, I was worried myself. Nas was a live wire, and if he ever felt threatened, he was going to dispose of whomever he felt the threat coming from. I shook my head at Junie, silently apologizing for what I was about to get his mother involved in. I considered taking Nas to another person, but if he found out it was all bullshit, then he would come at me.

"Look," I said as a glared at him, "She is ok. She's not fuckin' snitching; that's my word, Nas." He shot piercing, constant stares at me as I held his son. It was like I was putting his freedom in danger and for a split second, I felt he saw me as an enemy. I felt a shift coming from him that wasn't there before today. He leaned over and kissed Prince on the cheek and put his fitted hat back on as he stood up. I watched him walk to the door without acknowledging me, but before he left out, he spoke,

"Is he going over there tomorrow?"

"Yeah. I got some shit to take care of at a couple of the stash houses."

"No doubt," he said, walking out the door and letting it slam closed behind him. Prince jumped and spun around to look at me. I held him close, rocking back and forth. If I knew Nas like I know I did, this wasn't going to get any better until he was completely comfortable, and I honestly didn't even want to think about how that comfort was going to come about.

Chapter 5

"Hey, baby. Hey Mama's baby, are you ready to go to grandma's house? Are you?" I stood at the back seat of the car in front of Mrs. Butler's house, getting my last goodbyes in with Prince. As the days past, he looked more and more like a mix of Junie and Big Mama. His eyes were still as gray as they were on the day he was born and the dimple on his left cheek kept sinking into his face more and more. He was the cutest little boy I had ever laid my eyes on. The clouds above us were thick and dreary, and a light drizzle saturated the atmosphere. I looked up and down the block before I took him out of the car. The neighborhood was quiet as it had been since the days Junie and I came over here after school was out. We would grab a handful of candy from the penny candy store on the end of the block that was still there to this day. As we strolled down the sidewalk, he would make a beat with his mouth, and I would come in flowing right behind him. It was a perfect chemistry between us, which is probably why I just couldn't get him out of my head. Even though Nas was more of what I wanted, I couldn't deny the connection I had with Junie. Not even if I wanted to.

As I crept to the front door, I saw a black Impala roll to a stop right behind me. The drizzle from the sky fell down on me as I spun around, looking to see who was behind me. I sat Prince down and put my hand on my waist near the Glock that I kept on me for protection. Suddenly, the back door opened up, and Nas hopped out the back with all black attire on and a black fitted hat. I shook my head as he walked up to me,

"Nas, what the fuck are you doing here? You following me?"

"I just wanted to see who is watching my son during the day; you know what I'm sayin'? Something wrong with that? I can't see who is—"

"Fuck that shit, Nas. Prince been coming here for the past few months and you didn't give a shit about knowing who was watching him until I told you that shit a few days ago. You think I'm a dumb bitch or something?"

He smiled, both of his dimples alluring me as the rain began to fall down on his face. Ignoring me, he picked Prince up and headed to the door, pointing, "It's this one, right? Come on. Let's get my son out this rain and meet Mrs. Butler." I looked towards the car as Loc sat in the passenger's seat with the window partially cracked. I huffed, my breath visible in the air as it left my mouth. By the time I'd gotten to the door, Nas had already rang the bell, and Mrs. Butler was standing right there with a surprised look on her face. She made eye contact with me then she reached to open the door, stumbling as her hand missed the handle on the first try.

"Hi… Hi, Lyric. Hey Prince!" she said, smiling in an attempt to cover up any other emotions she felt at the moment. Nas walked in, looking around the front room as if he was admiring the décor. "This is a beautiful place, Mrs… Mrs. Butler, is it?" She grabbed the car seat from Nas, "Yes. Um, it's uhh…" I could tell she wanted to say Mom but she restrained herself, "it's Mrs. Butler. Why don't you two have a seat? I wasn't expecting um, the both of you." Nas looked over at me, smiling like the vicious killer that he was, and took a seat on the couch. Mrs. Butler sat down across from him, and I took a seat right in-between them. I didn't know if Nas remembered Mrs. Butler from the mall a while back but my guess was that he didn't. I'm not sure what his reaction would be if he knew he was sitting in the house of his biological parents. Mrs. Butler looked at me, searching for any clue where this was headed. I gave her a life line,

"Nas just wanted to come by and see who was watching his son while we were away."

She nodded as if she understood, "Oh, Ok. Well, I'm Mrs. Butler. I've known Lyric for umm… for quite some time now, you know? I've always considered her as a daughter to me so, by circumstance, I guess I will consider you… like a son."

"Nah, that's not necessary Mrs. Butler," he said. I glanced at her, and I could immediately tell that her heart broke into pieces when he said that. She could hide it from him, but not from me. Just then, Serena burst into the front room from the back, "Heeeeeey Prince!" she said, a big smile plastered across her face as she ran to him, "Hey Lyric, Hey…," she stopped, placing her hand over her mouth. Mrs. Butler and I looked at each other as Nas smiled, "And who is this?" he asked in a way that contradicted every inch of the thug inside of him. He stood up, extending his hand to her as she kept her mouth covered,

"Oh my God, is this… is this—"

I interrupted her, "Yes, this is Prince's Dad, Nas," I looked at him, "I've told all of them so much about you. They were just surprised to see you come by."

"Oh, you've told them so much about me, huh? Well, what exactly did you tell them, Lyric?" he said, venom dripping from his lips.

"Just how much you love Prince and how he just looks so much like you."

Serena sat down on the arm of the couch next to Mrs. Butler, looking back and forth between Nas and Prince. "Oh, that's it?" Nas stated as if I was leaving something out, "you didn't tell them how much of a good guy I am?" I put my hand on his leg, laughing to cover up the tense situation that was beginning to unfold, "Yes, you know I did. You have to be a good guy if you're helping me raise a son like this." He turned his attention towards Mrs. Butler as she held Prince, "We are a loving family, you know? I mean, I would hate if something were to happen to keep Lyric or me away from Prince. I mean, I don't know what I would do, you know? As a loving parent, you understand, don't you?" Mrs. Butler glanced at Nas curiously, "I understand completely. I also understand that I wouldn't do anything to cause my children to be taken away from me, and if I did, then I would just have to deal with the consequences."

My heart skipped a beat as Nas sat in his seat with an old, awkward smile on his face. Prince rocked back and forth on Mrs. Butler's lap, slobbering down his mouth without a care in the world. Serena sat quietly, glancing at Nas just to quickly look away whenever he turned towards her. I figured she was still processing everything that was unfolding in front of her. The tension in the front room reached its boiling point. Nas stood up abruptly as I mirrored his movement, standing between him and Mrs. Butler. I wasn't sure what he was going to do at that moment, but I wanted to be as much of a roadblock as I could if needed. He looked at me curiously, "Are you alright?" he pleasantly asked as he continued to contradict his true nature. "I'm good, I just... I was getting ready to walk you out because it looked like you were leaving." Mrs. Butler looked back and forth between us as if we were both crazy. The thing is, we both were, she just didn't know to what extent. He reached his hand out to Stacey,

"Well, Mrs. Butler, it was a pleasure to meet you finally."

"You as well."

"And the same to you, Serena. I'm sure I will see you two again you know, I mean, with Prince here and all."

"Please. Please do come back," Stacey said, "You are more than welcome anytime you want to come by. I would love for you to meet your... um, my husband."

"Oh, absolutely. I would love that. Now, you ladies have a wonderful day, alright?"

It was frightening how well he switched his demeanor in front of them. He reminded me of a schizophrenic or even worse, a sociopath who was considering killing his mother to keep her from talking. We walked outside into the pouring rain, he a few steps in front of me. "Nas!" I yelled as he kept walking at a brisk pace. I finally caught up with him and yanked on his arm, turning him around to face me,

"Nas, what the fuck was that, huh? Did you hear what you wanted to hear?"

"Yeah, I heard it and what I heard is that she is a fuckin' snitch."

"How did you even hear that?!"

"The fuckin' question is, how didn't you hear it?! You must've forgotten that we both killed muthafuckas that night, and if you ain't tryin' to tie up loose ends, then I probably got the wrong bitch by my side. You need to get yo' fuckin' priorities straight, Lyric. Now ain't the time to be bullshitting!"

He yelled as rain drops exploded all around us. Water fell from the bill of his fitted cap as the rain wet my hair, causing it to stick to my face. I looked at him, then back towards the house as Serena stood in the door. When I turned around, I heard a car door slam shut and just like that, he was gone. I stood in the rain for a few moments before I got in the car myself and left.

Later that day, I drove out to Allen-Bradley, the spot where Vinny worked. I texted him to let him know I was outside, and he came out on his lunch break to chill in the car with me. My hair and clothing were still wet from when I was outside talking to Nas.

"Damn, Lyric. What is the fuck you do? Take a shower in the rain and shit?"

"Nah. I was just talkin' to Nas in the worst place and shit."

"Oh," he looked at me, knowing something was wrong. Vinny wasn't "like" a brother to me; he was a brother. He could pick up on little shit like that about me even when I tried to hide it. "What's up, Lyric?"

"Nas is some bullshit, man. Some straight bullshit."

"What you mean?"

"You remember that Big Tuck shit?"

"Yeah."

"Well, I fucked around and told him that the police was startin' to look at us for that shit. But that ain't it; I told him who I heard it from."

"Ok… who did you hear it from?"

I sighed, "Mrs. Butler."

His mouth hung open, "Damn, Lyric. Fuck. Fuck. That shit is fucked," he paused, "Wait a minute, ain't that his mama? And Prince grandmama?"

"Hell yeah."

"Do he know that shit?"

"Nah. I mean, I told him a long ass time ago, but it seems like he forgot and shit. Even if I did tell him, I think the only thing it would do is piss him off even more."

"Fuck, Lyric. So, what he gon' do?"

"The nigga followed me to her spot this morning when I was dropping of Prince," he put his hand over his face as I continued speaking, "he went in and talked to her. The shit was mad awkward, though, you know what I'm sayin? I'm sittin' in there talking to the mother of a son I used to fuck with while her other son, who I am fucking with now, is in the front room, but the nigga doesn't even know that the woman he is talkin' to is really his mother." Vinny's eyes opened wide, seemingly confused at what I just said, "That's some fuckin' Jerry Springer ass shit if you ask me, Lyric." I laughed, "I mean, the shit ain't funny but you ain't lying. Fuck man, I know this nigga is gon' try some off the wall fuckin' shit. I can't even let that shit happen to her, though, you know what I'm sayin' Vinny? She ain't snitchin' on him or me. You know she ain't." He sighed, glancing out the window as the raindrops exploded when it made contact, "Yeah, but that nigga doesn't, and a nigga like that don't give a shit when his freedom is at risk. I already know."

We sat in the car silently for the next few minutes like we normally did when we were both hit with some heavy stuff and didn't know how to respond. Another silent conversation between us that only siblings could have with each other. The thunder grumbled above us as he turned to me, "You heard from Uncle Stew?" he asked, his eyebrows wrinkled up.

"Nah, why?"

"He ain't been in the crib since that day he said you came through. That was, what? A few days ago? Anyways, I saw him sleep in Big Mama room, and whenever he in there, I don't fuck with him, you know what I'm sayin? I mean, out of respect and shit, but I went to sleep that afternoon, and when I woke up the nigga was gone. Ain't seen him since."

"For real?"

"Yeah. I figured he just needed some time to himself or some shit, you know? So I didn't think nothing of it after the first day or so but it been a few days now, so I just figured I'd tell you about it."

"Aight. You good at the crib by yo'self?"

He laughed, "The fuck kind of question is that, Lyric? I'm a grown ass man. You think I'm scared to stay in the crib by myself?"

"I'm just sayin' I heard you scream when you told me you thought you saw Big Mama walking into the kitchen."

He laughed, "Fuck that shit, man. Them fuckin' spirits and shit? I don't fuck with them. You can't shoot that shit or nothing, and I did see enough of them in my life to know that I don't want to fuck with them. Ever."

I laughed, "Aight, nigga. I'ma let you get back to work, though."

"Aight. Hit me up, Lyric."

"Aight."

He got out of the car and ran through the rain back to his building. The shit on my mind was piling up by the second; first, this shit with Nas and Mrs. Butler had me worried for her life and preparing a way to keep her safe; second, Vinny just dropped this shit on me about Uncle Stew. I was hoping he didn't find his way back to the drugs because he was doing so well for so long without them. I would hate to see him go back, but I heard them relapses aren't nothing to fuck with. I could only hope and pray that he was alright, but I had my ear to the streets so I knew I could get a beat on him sooner or later.

The stash house was quiet. The niggas Nas put on were all on they shit, even in the rain. They had the fiends coming to them like clockwork every day. I pulled up to the curb and waved Peabody, one of the boys, over to my car. He was a young ass nigga, hard as fuck, though. He couldn't have been any more than 16-years-old, still had the baby face and everything, but the nigga carried himself like a grown ass man. He walked to the side of my car, his gold grill glimmering inside of his partially open mouth,

"What's good, Lyric?"

"Shit, you tell me? What's count?"

He pulled a roll out of his pocket, "This about $14,000 right here. Doobie got the rest of the dope over at his spot. You want me to grab him?"

"Nah, nah, you good. Give me that roll, though."

He handed it to me as he stood there in the rain, waiting for my next move. I unrolled the money, counting out $800 and giving it back to him, "Here, that's just for bein' the nigga you are right now, handling yo' business. You keep this shit up, we gon' put you over on the 21st street so you can put that shit in line over there." He took the money from my hand, "Aight, no doubt. I can handle that shit." I smiled, "Yeah, I know you can Lil' nigga. You runnin' this shit over here." He stood there with his hands in his pockets.

"Well aight," I said, "get back to it. Fuck with Nas or me if you need anything."

"Aight."

It was a short day for me. I only stopped at a few houses before I made my way to Big Mama's house, hoping to catch Uncle Stew over there. When I opened the door, the house was silent. The only noise being the buzz that came from the heater inside the house. I walked into Big Mama's room as the peace hit me immediately. "Hey, Big Mama," I said out loud, "if you could help me find Uncle Stew, we would appreciate it." I smiled, knowing that she heard me and hoped that she would lead me in the right direction. I left her room and walked down the stairs to the basement, the place where he slept. His room was a bit more cluttered than it usually was. His clothes were hanging out of his dresser, and the mattress on his bed was leaning a bit to the left. *This nigga needs to clean up*, I said to myself as I searched through his room. There was no sign of him, not even of the crossword puzzles he kept in bunches around the house. I shook my head and walked up the stairs and out the corner of my eye, I saw a tiny blue bag. I squinted my eyes and bent down to pick it up. It was packaged the same way Nas had ours put out. It was already opened and empty by the time I got to it, so I stuck my finger in there, hoping to get a taste of the residue. *This muthafucka!* I said to myself as I stormed up the stairs. *This nigga is getting high on our shit! I can't believe this!* I stormed through the kitchen and stood on the front patio, scanning up and down the block for any sign of him. It was the last thing I wanted to see—my uncle strung out on this shit again. I sent Vinny a text to let him know what was going on,

Yo, Unc on that shit again. Keep a lookout and we might need to change the locks. He gets bad enough, he gon' start trying to sell shit from out of the house. I'ma look for him. He responded a few moments later, *Aight, Lyric.*

For the rest of that day, I drove around the gutters, looking for anywhere that Uncle Stew could be—all of the usual crackhead hangout spots and soup kitchens, but I didn't see him anywhere. It was raining, though, so most of them found shelter somewhere, whether it was an abandoned building or under a bridge. He was strung out for a while, so my guess is that he knew many more places to hide than I did. Before I knew it, it was time to pick up Prince from Mrs. Butler's house, so I headed that way.

She opened the door. "Shhhh, the baby is sleep," she said as she ushered me in. I walked over to the couch where he was laid out on top of a blanket, his hand still clenching a bottle that was halfway gone. She smiled, "he was a handful today. Just restless, it seemed like, you know? It looked like something was bothering him and I wish he could talk to grandma so I could make him feel better," she glanced at him, "but he probably wouldn't tell me anyway, actin just like Junie." She caught herself. I knew that, in her mind, this was Junie's son and honestly, I was ok with her doing that. I knew there was just a void that Prince was going to fill for her, whether I liked it or not. I grabbed a few of his toys and placed them back inside of his baby bag, preparing to leave. She helped me for a minute before saying what was on her mind,

"You know, Lyric. Have you considered putting him up for adoption?"

I looked at her irrationally, "Uh, no. Never. Why?"

"Well," she was hesitant to go forward, but she did, "when Nas came by here earlier today? I knew he was bad news. I even told Serena that when you two left, and I know that you have a pretty tight bond with him. I'm just afraid that something will happen to Prince, you know? I mean, something will happen to you two first and then him. I understand that you two are grown and if I could lock you two away somewhere and keep you safe, I would. But Prince? He's just a baby, and we have to do everything in our power to keep him safe. He's not grown like you two so he can't make his deci—"

"Mom, I get what you're saying, and I understand where you're coming from, but honestly, adoption never crossed my mind. I mean, even when I was pregnant, and the doctors gave that option to me, I told them no. That is my baby and my baby is going to stay with me."

"But Lyric," she said, folding up his blankets, "are you sure he is safe? Are you positive?"

"How do you know he would be safe here, Mom?" She looked at me quizzically and in my mind, I thought about Nas's rage leading him to do something while Prince was here.

"I mean, I guess what I'm saying is, that danger is everywhere, and it could happen to anybody, no matter how much you try to keep things safe."

"I know, baby, I know. But the thing is, if you keep yourself out of trouble then most likely, trouble won't find you. You've just gotta keep yourself clear from it. Respect danger and it will respect you."

"Look, Mom. I truly appreciate your concern for Prince; I really do, but I'm not going to give him up for adoption. Not to you or anybody else," I put a few more things in his bag, "now, God forbid, if something happens to me then yes, please PLEASE take care of Prince for us. I mean, I already know you would but until that happens, Prince will be staying with his parents, ok?"

She sighed. I knew she had a deep fear for his safety, and she had a good reason for it. As me and Nas were growing our empire, we were becoming bigger targets for somebody to knock us off our throne just like Nas did to Big Tuck. It was a vicious cycle in the drug game, but we knew what we were getting into from the jump, so it wasn't a surprise to us. The thing is, I was just as worried about her safety as she was for mine. A part of me wanted to tell her to leave town for a while until some things blow over but just knowing the type of woman she was, I knew she wasn't going to budge. She was tough and honestly, I could see glimpses of her strength in Nas. I put Prince in his car seat; he was still sound asleep, and I kissed Mrs. Butler on the cheek. She was uneasy, but she hugged and kissed me back. I covered Prince as we walked out into the pouring rain—a perfect visual of what my life was becoming.

Chapter 6

Nas didn't come home that night, so after I dropped Prince off the next day, I drove over to the central spot on Buffum Street. The house was pretty quiet on the outside, just a few men hanging around the front door. They all nodded their heads at me, the quiet way most people said, "What's up." The front door was bolted shut, and when I knocked, I could hear the person on the other end removing them before he opened the door. When I walked through, Man-Man stood with a shotgun clenched in his hand.

"Whassup Lyric?"

"Hey, Man-Man. You aight?"

"I'm good."

He bolted the door back as I walked through the house. The furniture was gone out of the front room, making the wooden floors clearly visible. All of the rooms on the first floor were cleaned out. I turned to Man-Man,

"Where the fuck is everybody?"

"They moved all that shit to the basement. It was too much in the open up here, and Nas had some work done. I'll take you down there."

He walked me over to the basement door and knocked three times, paused, and then hit twice. A few more bolts were removed from that door, and we walked down the basement stairs. All the women were down there, bagging coke like an assembly line. They hired a few men since the last time I came through, and they were all topless. The hypes would try to sneak drugs out in their clothing, so Nas would make them all work naked until it was time for them to go. He figured he had enough bodies on him already, and he was tired of killing people for stealing. "A fuckin' hype is gon' be a fuckin' hype, so shit, we'll just make them strip till they leave." Those were his words and he stood by them. Man-Man took me to the edge of the basement, showing me a trap door.

"If we get raided, they been trained to throw all the shit in here. They will never find it once it goes in."

When he closed it, there was no sign of a door ever being there. It was the perfect cover up for the drug operation we had going on. Nas was always trying to stay a few steps ahead of the police, and I had to admit, with something like this, he was guaranteed to be ahead of them if the time ever came. I eventually made my way back upstairs after the brief tour and walked to Nas's room. *Knock, Knock.*

"Who that?"

"It's Lyric."

I heard some rustling behind the door and then he finally opened it for me to come in. "Whassup, Ma?" he said, kissing me on the cheek and closing the door behind me. I walked over to the bed and took a seat, "Shit. I'm chillin. You good?" He walked over and took a seat right next to me before answering,

"I'm straight. Straighter than a muthafucka."

"You know you were on some bullshit the other day, right?"

"When?"

"Don't play dumb, nigga. When you followed me to Mrs. Butler's house."

"Oh, that shit?" he laughed, "ain't nobody thinkin' 'bout that bitch," he said, avoiding eye contact with me.

"Why she gotta be a bitch?"

He turned around to face me, "Oh shit, my bad. I forgot that was like yo' other Moms and shit, my bad yo. Um, ain't nobody thinkin' about that broad. Now, is that better?"

"Whatever, Nigga."

I stood up and walked over to the window. The dogs barked as they wrestled with each other in the grass, behaving as if they were trying to rip each other's head off. I could hear them growling as they went back and forth. Nas came up behind me, squeezing me around my waist, "My bad, Ma. I am not tryin' to piss you off or nothin' but um, Mrs. Butler is old news now. Ain't nobody thinkin' about her." I turned towards him, "You promise?" He smiled, still avoiding eye-contact with me, "I promise baby, I promise. I ain't gon' touch that old lady." I'd known him for almost two years now, and one thing I knew is when he wasn't honest, but right now, I couldn't get a good read on him. I just decided to trust what he told me because I didn't believe he would hurt a woman that his son was so fond of. I lifted myself on my tiptoes to kiss him on the lips,

"Ok, baby. I'll believe you."

"Word. So, what you think about moving to another city?"

"Another city? I don't know, Nas. I mean, we good here, ain't we?"

"We good here and shit, but this world is bigger than Milwaukee. I'm tryin' to set up shit in multiple cities so I can keep building the empire, you know what I'm sayin'?"

"Yeah, but shit, where you tryin' to go?"

"We can stay around here. Detroit. Chicago. Shit, I'd even consider Minnesota."

"I don't know, baby."

"What's the problem?"

"I mean, Prince for one. We'd have to find another sitter, and I don't wanna leave my baby with just anybody."

"Trust me, Ma. All that shit will be taken care of. Just trust ya' man on this one, aight?"

"Shit Nas, I gotta think about it."

I left his arms and walked back over to the bed as he stood at the window for a few moments. I knew he wouldn't want to stay here in Milwaukee for a long time. In about two years, he had pretty much come here and done what he set out to do. On top of that, nobody, not even the police were on to him yet except for Big Tuck's murder, but they hadn't spoken to either one of us about it. As far as we were concerned, that case was going to be a cold file. He finally walked over and sat next to me on the bed, rubbing his hand up and down my thigh, "Ma, just trust me, aight? I'm going to make sure you and Prince are straight. Y'all my life, you know what I'm saying? I ain't gon' do shit that will have y'all in danger. I'm going to make sure mine is safe every time before I jump off into anything, you should know that. I want you to know that if you don't." He held my cheek in his hand, guiding me to look him in the eye.

"You trust me?" he asked with a look of confidence.

I sighed, "Yeah baby, I trust you." He smiled, "that's what I like to hear."

He leaned over and kissed me on the neck once, and I put my hand on the back of his head. He went in for another kiss, except this time, he used his tongue to make a line from my neck to the tip of my ear. I leaned backward on the bed as he slowly climbed atop of me, ripping the buttons off my shirt as he pulled it open. I was immediately moist from his aggression as he pulled my bra down and put my breast in his mouth, licking my nipples back and forth with his tongue. He slid down lower, kissing my stomach as he loosened my pants and pulled them down. A moment later, I felt his tongue inside of me. I didn't remember the last time he gave me head, but I wouldn't forget this time. He licked my clit slow at first and then sped up before he put his face all the way in it. I wrapped my legs around his head as he grabbed my thighs, the fullness of his tongue all over my pussy. I grabbed his head, pushing him in deeper as I heard him slurping me, which turned me on even more. "I'm about to cum," I said, pushing his head deeper inside as he slowly stroked my clit with his tongue. My legs locked around him and as I came, my whole body shook from pleasure. After I had released him, he took his pants off, exposing his erection. He scooted up to my head and shoved his dick into my mouth, and I took all of it, bobbing my head on it back and forth as he stroked my wet pussy with his hand. Suddenly, he pushed my head back and scooted down lower, inserting his meat into my vagina hard, pounding me like he was punishing me for something I did wrong. I wanted him to hurt me, though. I wanted him to stick his fat ass dick inside of me so deep that it hurt when I tried to walk. He pinned my legs back and went in as I moaned, a sound mixed with pleasure and pain. He put his hand around my throat, squeezing it just tight enough to where I felt him but I didn't pass out. I glanced in the mirror, watching him pump me without mercy until he stopped and grabbed my legs, flipping me over onto my stomach. He used so much strength that I couldn't have stopped him if I wanted to. Before I could say anything, I felt his dick deep inside my pussy while he stuck a thumb in my ass and it was at that moment that I came again. He smacked my ass while I gripped the pillow so hard that it broke one of my nails. He grabbed me and pushed his dick in as deep as it could go as the pain caused so much pleasure that I couldn't make out which one it was. Moments later, I felt his cum shoot inside of me.

I flopped down on the bed as he lay down next to me, breathing hard and trying to catch his breath. I curled up and scooted right next to him as we both laid on the bed naked until we fell asleep. Whatever doubts I had about moving out of town with him were gone now. He sealed the deal with that one fuck he gave and reminded me of how sprung I was over him. Who was I kidding? There was no way in the world I was going to let him leave this city without me.

When I woke up, he was already gone. The sun was just beginning to go down outside as I reached for my phone to look at the time: 5:52 pm. I was late picking up Prince, so I knew I had to get over there before it was too late. I had two text messages, both from Vinny: *Lyric, Uncle Stew came back home, and that nigga is on that shit. Come through when you can. Fuck*, I said to myself, *got-damn it!* I scrolled to the next message, *Yo, Lyric; I almost had to square up with this nigga. He tried to snake me for my PS4. I had to swing on him. Come through.* I picked up my phone, ready to throw it into the wall but I restrained myself. I couldn't believe what I had just read. *I'm on my way, Vinny,* I messaged right back.

I came to Big Mama's house as Vinny stood on the front porch as if he was waiting for Uncle Stew to try to come back. He was shaking his head, apologizing as soon as I stepped out my car,

"Yo, my bad Lyric, my bad. I had to, though. That nigga was literally on some other shit. I mean, this nigga—"

"Vinny, Chill. I already know how he can get."

I walked inside the house to look around, "Yo, did he take anything else?" He locked the door behind him, "Nah, I mean. I didn't check anywhere else but the front room and the kitchen and shit. I didn't go in Big mama's room, though. You know I don't fuck with her room." As soon as he said that, I thought about the picture of my mom that Big Mama kept in a gold frame. "Shit!" I said out loud as I ran to the room. The picture frame was gone, the glass that held my mother's picture in was broken into pieces on the dresser. I walked over to the picture, moving the glass off of it as I glanced at my mother. She had the same, solemn look on her face as if she knew what her brother just did. I left the room in a hurry and went back to the front.

"How long has he been gone?"

He looked down at his watch, "I don't know. Maybe like an hour or two."

"Did he have a bike or anything?"

"He rolled off on a bike now that I think about it."

"Which way did he go?"

"He went to the left."

"Aight. Aye, beat the shit out of him if he comes back again, but this time don't let him leave until I get here. I don't give a fuck what time it is."

"Aight, but yo' Lyric, them fuckin' crackheads be havin' like super human strength sometimes when they get high. They are—"

"Vinny, shut the fuck up."

The streetlights flickered on as I got in my car and headed down the block. I could narrow it down by knowing which way he went when he left the house. In this direction, there were some crack houses and soup kitchens scattered throughout the area. It was a nice evening, so he was bound to be hanging around one of those spots. I got out my car and walked into one of the abandoned houses with my pistol drawn, "Where the fuck is Stew at?" I yelled, aiming the gun at a house full of hypes. They all scattered out the room like roaches when the lights are turned on, leaving behind crack pipes and alcohol bottles. "Stew!" I yelled out, walking through the house with my pistol out, ready to fire at anything that charged at me. He wasn't there, so I got in my car and headed to the next spot. It was the same outcome as fiends jumped out of first-story windows just to get away from me. I walked to the backyard and caught a woman giving head to another man by a fence. He looked over at me, his beard full of lint, the whites of his eyes looked as if he had jaundice. They didn't even stop what they were doing, she kept sucking his dick as he leaned against the fence, a few other crackheads laying down with a clear view of them as if they were watching a live porno. I spun around and left, knowing that there weren't many more places around here where I would find him.

The soup kitchen was one of the last spots I was going to have time to go to tonight. I had already called Mrs. Butler and let her know something came up so I was running late, but now I was over two hours past the time I was supposed to be there. I knew she didn't mind keeping him longer than she was scheduled to, but I didn't want to come off as a neglectful mother. I walked into the soup kitchen as one of the workers cleaned up the tables. They had just fed a group of homeless people not too long before I showed up. "Hey," I said, trying to get her attention. She turned around; her hair wrapped up in a navy blue bandana as crow's feet stretched to the corner of her eyes. She looked as if she was thirty going on fifty. "Do you know somebody by the name of Stew?" She put her towel down, focusing her eyes on me,

"Stew? Um, does he have the last name?"

"Stewart Sutton."

"Hmmm," she said rubbing her chin, "No, I don't recall. Can you describe him to me?"

"He's tall. A few inches taller than me, real slim. He's missing a lot of teeth on his top and bottom rows. He has a—"

"Scar right below his chin, right? And he has some of the prettiest gray eyes that I've ever seen on an addict. Yup, I know him. I sho' do."

"Has he been here?"

"You just missed him not too long ago. He came in here to get a bite to eat and then he left again. I never thought I would see him strung out again," she said, placing used dishes inside her blue bin, "but he is, and he looks worse off than he did before."

"Do you know which way he went?"

"No, now I don't know that. He did say he was tired, though, and he wanted to catch some sleep. Not too many places around here for that, though, so there ain't no tellin', really."

I sighed, "Thank you, ma'am."

"No problem, sugar. Now, I hope you find him and get him some help. He made too much progress to fall back down into the pit again. It's a shame, it is."

I left the soup kitchen and drove up and down city blocks, scanning every homeless person for their features to see if it was Uncle Stew. I had driven for about thirty minutes before I got a text from Vinny,

Yo, he's here. I see him out back by the garage. It looks like he is sleep but he isn't trying to get in or nothing. He's just lying there on the ground.

I responded, *I'll be there in like 5 minutes.*

I sped back to Big Mama's house and parked a few spots down so he wouldn't hear me pull up in the driveway and have a chance to run. I crept up in between Big Mama's house and her neighbors and that's when I saw him, laid out on the ground on top of some cardboard with a dirty ass blanket thrown across him. I gradually walked up to him, being careful not to make a sudden noise to wake him up. When I was close, I kicked him in his side. He yelled out in agony as I kicked him again and again until he begged me to stop,

"Lyric! Please! Stop! Stop!"

"Fuck you, Stew! You ain't supposed to be like this no more!"

I kicked him again as he backed up against the garage, doing his best to absorb the blows I was giving him. "What the fuck is wrong with you?" I said as tears fell from his eyes. His lips were white and cracked like cement in the winter, bags under his eyes were noticeable, even in the dark alley.

"I'm sorry, Lyric! I'm sorry!"

"The fuck you mean, you sorry!? You sorry for what?! For turning into a fuckin' hype again, huh!? For takin' my mama frame and selling it for dope!? Is that what you sorry for?!"

"Yes! Yes!" he yelled out with his hands up, preparing to protect himself from more of my attacks, "I'm sorry for all of it, Lyric! I'm sorry!"

I balled my fist up, ready to strike him in the head as he leaned further away from me, silently begging me not to continue. His arms were exposed, I saw dark blue and purple marks where he stuck needles in his veins—the bruises from using his body in a way it was never meant to be used. His fingernails were dirty, looking as if he hadn't had a bath in weeks. I stepped back and buried my head in my hands. It usually took a lot to break me, and I hadn't cried since Big Mama died of cancer but this time, I felt death again. It seemed like the Uncle Stew I had grown to know and love had died, and now, the crackhead in front of me was who replaced him. I calmed down, leaning against the garage wall and sliding down to where he was sitting. The tears that fell out my eyes mirrored his,

"How, Stew? How the fuck did you get back like this?"

He wiped his eyes, "I... I don't know, Lyric. I was just... I was laying in Mama's room the day after you left and I dropped some of my peppermints onto the floor. When I reached down there to get them, I pulled up a couple of baggies of crack. I didn't put them there, Lyric! I promise I didn't, but they were just there… and the temptation was too much for me to resist. I mean, the reason I got clean before was that I wasn't around it, you know? And if I ever was, I wasn't alone but this time I was alone. I was all by my fucking self, and I took that crack out of Mama's room, went downstairs, and I got high. I got high and from that day, I didn't look back."

As he spoke, I thought about the last time I was at Big Mama' house, laying in her bed. I remembered taking the gun and baggies out of my waistband and sitting them on the floor, but I only remembered taking the gun back with me. *Did I forget about the crack?* I thought to myself as Uncle Stew went on, crying and explaining himself even further. A sickening feeling went to the pit of my stomach once I realized that the crack I left there accidentally was the crack that got him addicted again. I turned towards him; his face was devoid of the life he had for the past year. His eyes were as if the light he held was snuffed out. I beheld him, and all I could think about was that it was my fault. I reached over to embrace him, and he was hesitant to hug me back for the first few moments, then he eventually gave in and put his arms around me. "I'm sorry, Lyric. I did my best, hear. Tell mama I did my best." I wiped tears from my eyes and held him even tighter. For some reason, I felt this was the end for him, and I only felt that way because I could sense that he had given up.

"Uncle Stew," I said, "You gotta fight this, ok? You can't quit. That is not who you are anymore. You're not this… this hype that you think you are."

"No, Lyric. Baby, this is me. This is Stewart, the old dingy crack nigger that ain't gonna never amount to anything in life. You know, Mama was right when she said that back then. I am not gonna never amount to nothing, and I'm as good as dead. I am."

"Unc, come on man, just stay with me. I'm going to go and get you something to eat, ok? Until then, just come in the house. Just chill."

"No, no, no. I already went in there once actin' a fool and little brother hit me square in the mouth. I deserved it, though, I did. I was going out of control because I needed a fix. That's when I went in Mama's room and," he paused, fighting back tears, "and broke the gold frame that had yo mama's picture in it. I just broke the frame and left the glass on the dresser, and I know it broke Mama's heart! I just know it did!" he said as he burst out into cries that were inconsolable, "I ain't shit, Lyric! I ain't shit!"

"Unc, come on," I said, reaching for his hand as I stood up.

"No, Lyric. No, and I mean, no! I don't deserve to be in that house. I don't deserve to be around y'all. I fucked up, and I'm done, you hear me? I'm done!"

"Unc, ok. Just wait right here, ok? I'm going to go and talk to Vinny. Just wait and I'm gonna have some food for you when I come back, ok?"

I turned around to rush to the house as he called out to me, "Lyric, just know that the time we spent together as a family was something I always wanted. I always wanted to know my niece and patch things up with my mama before anything happened to us. The Good Lord saw fit for me to do that and now, I'm back where I belong. I love you, ok?"

"Uncle Stew, I love you too, but I'll be right back, ok? Just hold tight."

I ran inside the house and fixed him a sandwich as quickly as I could and ran back outside to the back. "Uncle Stew, here you… Uncle Stew?" I looked around the garage for him, but he was gone. His blanket and the cardboard he laid on wasn't there either so I knew he had left. I threw the sandwich into the garage door as the insides exploded back onto the ground. The cries I made could have been heard a few houses down as the pain of regret and sorrow became too much to bear. Vinny came outside moments later. "Lyric? You okay?" he asked, bending down to me as I went to my knees in tears. "It's all my fault," I yelled as he tried to console me. "It's all my fuckin' fault that he's like that! It's my fault!" I screamed it at the top of my lungs as Vinny squeezed me as tight as he could, still trying to understand why it was my fault. "It's ok, Lyric. It's gonna be alright," he said as he sat on the cement, rocking me back and forth.

Eventually, he got me to come inside the house, and that's when I told him everything that happened. He didn't say anything to condemn me, he just shook his head and kept saying, "Damn, we gotta help him. We gotta help him." I admired the way he felt that helping was something we both had to do. He never made me feel like it was all my fault that Uncle Stew was strung out again even though it was all my fault. There was nothing we could do for him, though. Uncle Stew was going to do what was best for him, and I knew he wasn't going to come back around to the house. He was too ashamed to show his face here again, but all I could do was pray that he would be alright. That night, I slept in Big Mama's bed for a little while before I left. I didn't have any dreams of her or my mom that time either, and I thought it was weird that I didn't since I had them every other time, but if I had to guess, I knew why. I knew it was because I had gotten their son and brother strung out because of stupid ass decisions I made with my life. I started to think about what Mrs. Butler said about Prince and keeping him safe. I didn't try to hurt Uncle Stew and in the same sense, I could do things that hurt Prince when it wasn't even my intention to do so. Maybe I did need to let them adopt him because if I kept being careless as I was now, I knew something bad could happen to him.

I didn't get to Mrs. Butler's house until about 10 pm. She was getting Prince ready for bed and by the time I showed up, she was dressed in a housecoat with a scarf tied around her head.

"Girl, why are you comin' out here this time of night?" she asked, flipping on the porch light so I could see my way into the house.

"I'm sorry, Mom, I just got tied up in an emergency."

I walked past her as she caught a glimpse of my bloodshot eyes, "Lyric, you been crying? What's wrong, baby?" I wiped my eyes, "Nothing. I mean, it's just Big Mama's side of the family, you know? Some stuff happened with my Uncle." She looked concerned, but I didn't have the strength to talk about it anymore. Allen walked into the room moments later with Prince, showing off the matching pajamas he bought for the two of them. I could see the sadness on his face when he realized I was here to take him home, "Aw man," he said, "I thought we were going to get to keep him for the night." I smiled the best I could, "I'm sorry, Dad. I would have left him, but I need to just hold him for the night. When I have him, I feel like all my problems mean nothing anymore because he is with me." He smiled, "Trust me, I know the feeling. I definitely know the feeling. Well, let me help you take him out. I know this boy is a monster to deal with when he's being carried in that car seat." Allen went back to the room to get the rest of his things.

When he left, I whispered to Mrs. Butler, "Listen, I think I might take you up on that offer."

"What offer?"

I took a deep breath, "Adopting Prince. I think it might be the best thing for him right now, I mean, at least for the time being."

Her eyes widened as if I said something she never expected to hear, "Are you sure, Lyric?"

"Yes, I'm sure. I just... I think he would be safer here. It's just temporary, though, you know? I mean, I'm not actually living a life suitable to keep him safe right now."

"Ok, honey. Um, did you talk to Nas?"

"No."

She paused. "Well, you need to talk to him about it first, ok? He's going to have to sign off on this arrangement, too." I knew that would be easier said than done as Allen walked back into the front room with Prince all bundled up. "Ok, he's ready to go, Mommy. I bet he will fall asleep as soon as you drive off this block." I reached in and kissed him on the cheek and then followed Allen outside. Mrs. Butler grabbed my arm before I left the house and pulled me in for a hug, "I love you, baby, ok? Don't you ever forget that? You will ALWAYS be my daughter-in-law, no matter what happens and Prince is your child, ok? He is YOURS, and as far as I'm concerned, all we are here to do is help when you need it," she kissed me on my cheek, "I love you, ok? And I'm praying for you." I felt the warmth from her hug. It was something I needed more than anything at the moment. "Thank you and I love you too, Mom."

That night, I hoped that Nas would come home so I could talk to him about Prince. I knew he would have been against it if I brought it up to him a few months ago, but now it seemed like it was the best time, especially with him talking about moving away to another city. I wanted Prince to be somewhere stable where he would have a normal life. School, friends, even some after-school activities like athletics. As far as I'm concerned, he could be the next Kobe Bryant so I wanted to give him every chance for that to happen.

Nas never came home, though, and it was another lonely night with me inside of a big, four-bedroom house that I didn't even need. Even though Prince was cuddled next me sound asleep, I felt the loneliest I had in years.

Chapter 7

When I got to their house, police lights lit up the block as they were parked in front of her house. I pulled up as close as I could in my car before I leaped out and ran to their home. Police officers stood in front of me, blocking my path. "That's my mother!" I yelled out frantically as I tried to move them away from me.

"Ma'am, just calm down. We're—"

Just then, Serena ran down towards me and caught hold of my arm, pulling me past them with tears in her eyes. "What happened?" I yelled as she wiped tears from her eyes, pulling me closer to the house. Inside, three police officers glared at me when I walked through the door as they stood in front of Stacey. She was clearly shaken up as she rocked back and forth on her couch, her lip burst and swollen. I walked up to her, "Mom? Mom, what happened? Where is Dad?" I said as my heart beat through my chest. Her eyes locked on mine as she stood up and embraced me, her tears dripping down onto my shoulder. She tried to talk, but she couldn't squeeze the words out because of her tears. I looked at the officers,

"What's going on here? What happened to my mother?"

The short, round officer looked at me incredulously, "Attempted murder," he said as he rocked back and forth on his heels, "And who are you?" I turned back to Mrs. Butler, "I'm her daughter," I said as I held her tighter. Serena sat on the couch, the same horrified look on her face I saw when she ran towards me outside. The officers turned to her, "Ma'am, you say you didn't see anything? You just heard it, right?" She answered robotically, "Yes. I just heard it; I didn't see his face. I heard him; I just didn't see him." The officer wrote a few things down before he addressed Mrs. Butler again,

"Ma'am, anything you can tell us will be helpful, ok?"

"I've told you. He wore a mask, and he made like he was going to snatch my purse, but then he let it go and struck me with his pistol. When I fell to the ground, he stood over me and aimed it directly at my head and pulled the trigger but the gun jammed. He called me a bitch, and then he pulled it three more times, and it just clicked, no bullets came out. That's when Serena yelled my name and then he took off down the street. When he stood next to me, he was a few inches taller than me, and he was a skinny guy, not big at all. That's all I know. That's all I can tell you."

The officer turned towards his partners as they mumbled some things between them that I couldn't make out from where I stood. I held her in my arms tightly as she kept crying, Serena rocking back and forth in the same position. I couldn't help but think about Nas right now. The person she described fit Man-Man's description to perfection. His height, his build and on top of that, he was in the car with him when they came over here a few days ago. *He promised*, I thought to myself as my anger was on a steady incline as soon as I heard Mrs. Butler's story. I let her go and said,

"Mom, I'm gonna be back to check on you, ok?"

"Wait, baby, where is Prince?"

"I don't think he should stay here today, Mom. I mean, you're a not in—"

"Please, just bring him in. If anything, he is going to help me keep my mind off what just happened. Your father should be on his way home so he'll be here with us. Please, Lyric? Just… just bring him. Please."

I couldn't look her in the eyes and still tell her no, especially the way she was pleading with me. I could see in her eyes that he was the little bit of hope that she could hold onto right now, and I know what that meant for her. Prince was still in the car fast asleep when I walked back outside. I knew that there were police cars all around us that could pose as temporary babysitters while I ran inside. I brought him in, and he was awakened as soon as he heard Mrs. Butler's voice. His dimple pushed his cheek in as he flailed his arms, trying to free himself from the car seat. "There is my baby!" she said, smiling at him as she unbuckled his safety belts. Serena got up and walked over to him, kissing him on his face as he cooed for them to keep going.

"I'll be back in a few hours, ok, Mom?"

"Ok, sweetie. You be careful out there, ok?"

I left the house in a heartbeat and headed straight to the trap house on Buffum Street. I had tunnel vision as I drove, focused on Nas as I subconsciously avoided potholes and sped through yellow lights before they turned red. I wasn't going to stop if I didn't have to. I parked outside the house and jumped out the car. A few men nodded at me as they stood outside but I walked right past them in a blur and started banging on the door, "Open this fuckin' door, Loc!" He waited for a few moments as I hit it again and the bolts were removed from the other side one by one. As soon as he cracked it, I kicked it the rest of the way open. Loc jumped back with his shotgun aimed at me, but I paid no attention to it. "Where is Nas at, Loc?" I asked, an ice grill plastered on my face. "He's gone. He left earlier this morning, and he hasn't been back since. He took Man-Man with him somewhere." "That bitch ass nigga", I said out loud, "he fucking promised! He promised me!"

I spun around and went back to my car, thinking for a moment where he could be. *It's Tuesday*, I thought to myself, *that muthafucka is down at the stash house on third.* He kept his pattern of travel sporadic to keep niggas from jumping out on him because they knew where he would go but from the beginning, he told me where he would be on certain days, and I could only hope that he stuck to it. I pulled up to the spot and parked right behind his truck. A few fiends walked around the neighborhood like zombies as I waited for him to come outside. One of the dope boys walked up to my car,

"Yo, what's good, Lyric?"

"Shit. Nas in there, ain't he?"

"Yeah. You want me to get him for you?"

"Nah, you good. I'ma just wait on him myself."

"Aight then."

He walked away from my car, his pants sagging just below his ass. I switched my attention back to the door and after a few minutes, it didn't appear that he was coming right out, so I got up and headed inside. He was in the backroom with Man-Man, making a count of the money they had back there. "Lyric, whassup Ma?" he said, reaching for a kiss. I put my hands on his chest and pushed him backward. He strumbled a little bit before he put his arm up, bracing himself against the wall, saying, "Lyric, what the fuck is wrong with you?" I stepped to him again and pushed him.

"What you mean what the fuck is wrong with me?! You promised me you weren't gon' do nothing to her! You promised me!"

"Whoa, what the fuck you talking about? Shit. Calm yo' ass the fuck down!"

"Nah, fuck you, you bitch ass nigga! That woman is like a mother to me! She watches Prince, and you just gon' fuckin' try to kill her?! Bust her fuckin' lip over some shit I told you not to even worry about?!"

The surprised look on his face faded away and was immediately replaced with the glare he had before he committed a murder. It didn't put an ounce of fear into me though because I had the same look. The same capability he dead and if it came to it, we would just be two dead muthafuckas in a stash house.

"Look, I told you I wasn't gon' touch her and I didn't. You got the wrong nigga right now."

"Bullshit, muthafucka! The nigga she described was Man-Man!"

Nas looked over at him, then back towards me, "Look, and I'm trying to keep my peace here with yo' ass, if some fucked up shit happened to that bitch, I didn't have nothing to do with it. Man-Man didn't have anything to do with it, aight? You barkin' up the wrong tree, and you need to take yo' ass somewhere before I knock the shit out of you. Don't fuckin' come chargin' me up about some bullshit that you think I did. Betta get the fuck from around here," he said, brushing me off as he went back to count the money. I picked up a wooden board that laid against the wall and smacked him across the back of the head with it. He stumbled forward into the table the money was on as Man-Man came from behind me and snatched the board out of my hand, damn near knocking me to the ground. Nas rubbed the back of his head with his hand, checking it to see if there was blood. He slowly spun around to me, his rage boiling inside of him. He walked up to me as I squared up, "Bitch, if you ever in yo' mutha fuckin' life hit me with anything else, I will fuckin' kill you." Suddenly, before I could react, he reached and put his hands around my throat, choking me harder than he did when we had sex. I put my hands over him, trying to break free from his grasp but he was much too strong for me. He backed me into a wall, squeezing tighter as I felt myself blacking out. If it wasn't for Man-Man coming to pull him off of me, I think I would have died right there. Nas let me go as I fell backward, smacking my head into the wall on my way down, gasping for air.

Nas stood over me, shaking his head, "I told yo' ass I didn't have shit to do with that bitch, but if you wanna keep bein' Captain save-a-bitch, you go ahead. I'll tell you this, though, if you find yourself dead, don't say I didn't warn you." He picked up the bag of money and walked out the room, leaving me against the wall. Man-Man had glanced towards me before he left, not saying a word. We were so much alike that it was crazy, and I thought that would be the glue that kept us together, but as time passed, I started to realize that being exactly like your partner is never good in a relationship. If one is crazy, the other needs to be mellow. If one is a serious, then the other one needs to be hilarious. It's just how life works; opposites attract, and I was beginning to see how Nas would never be able to compare to Junie when the whole time, I thought it was the other way around.

After a few moments, I got up and left the stash house. I was headed back to Mrs. Butler's house before I got the urge to stop at Big Mama's cemetery. I hadn't been there in a while because her room was just the same to me. I stopped to pick up a few flowers on my way, knowing that the ones I dropped off a while back were no longer good. The cemetery was quiet when I showed up, not another car in sight as I walked to her grave somberly as if I was reburying her myself. A gust of wind blew as soon as I stopped at her headstone, "Hannah Big Mama Tucker," I said to myself with a smile. The headstone was cold against my back as I sat down on it, placing the flowers next to me.

"Hey, Big Mama. Stuff has been crazy these past few months, but I know you see it. I… I just want to apologize for what I did to Uncle Stew. I just…"

"Baby, he is a grown man. You can't hold yourself accountable for what he did."

The voice was so clear that it caused me to jump and look around to see if anybody was next to me. That's how real it felt when I heard her voice. Maybe it was my imagination placing her there with her voice, but whatever it was, I listened.

"But Big Mama, I put the drugs there."

"Yeah, you did. And I can't believe you had the nerve to have drugs AND a gun in Big Mama's house. What is wrong with you, girl?!"

"It's just... it's just my life right now, Big Mama. I didn't expect it to be this way; it's just where I am."

"Listen, Stewart is capable of handling himself so you can't allow that to weigh you down. Yes, you had the drugs in my house, but you didn't force him to take them. He did it on his own, and he will be held accountable for his actions, not you. But I'll tell you this, that boy Nas? You need to get away from him. Just look at your life. You were rapping and doing something positive before he came along. Let me ask you, when was the last time you performed on stage?"

"I don't remember."

"Umm-hmm, ok. And when was the last time you did something for Nas?"

"Like every day."

"You see there? I don't even have to point it out. That boy has you wrapped around his finger, and it's a shame what he did to Mrs. Butler."

I stood up as if she was right in front of me, "You know he did it?" I asked anxiously. "Child, even you know he did it. That boy is dangerous, you hear? Just be careful down there, Lyric. The Lord has patience for you, but you won't even reach your potential if you die before your time because of foolishness. The Lord can hear and speak to you just like I can; you just have to put yourself in a position to understand him."

"Ok, Big Mama," I said, "Do you think I should let Mrs. Butler adopt Prince? Big Mama?"

A gust of wind swept over me as I waited for an answer that would never come. I don't know if I imagined the whole thing or if it happened, either way, I knew something had to change between Nas and me. Something had to give because, at the rate we were going now, one of us wasn't going to make it out alive, and I was damn sure the person left breathing was going to be me. I kissed her headstone and made my way back to my car as the sun occasionally peeked through the thick, white clouds above. I sat in my car for a few moments, thinking about my next moves. I remembered when Nas mentioned he wanted to get out of town. *Maybe I could leave without him*, I thought to myself. Just then, I got a text from Mrs. Butler,*Hey, sweetie, can you let me know when you're on your way? I want to get something to eat, but your dad won't let any of us leave the house right now. He's got us all on lockdown, lol.*

Sure Mom, just tell me what you want. I'm on my way right now.

If Nas was going to hurt either one of them, he was going to have a fight on his hands, but I prayed that it didn't come to that point. I prayed with everything I had in me and if God were as real as Big Mama said he was, then right now would be the perfect time to show me.

Chapter 8

It was nearly 1 am when he walked through the door. I heard him rustling around downstairs before he made his way up to our room. He had a glassy look in his eyes as he stumbled on his way to my bed. When he flopped down, I smelled the liquor on his breath immediately. His hands began roaming over my body as I laid there, motionless. Moments later, he ripped my underwear down off my waist and stripped naked, pushing himself inside of me. "Wait," I said as he pushed into it deeper, but he disregarded my plea. I looked over at Prince as he lay asleep on the other side of my king-sized bed. I was completely detached to Nas as he fucked me and this was the first time it had ever been that way. After what he did to Mrs. Butler and the way he choked me back at the stash house, I couldn't understand how he could make his way over here like nothing was wrong. "Ohhh, shit Ma," he said as he stroked me fast with my legs wide open. I did my best not to move as much so we wouldn't wake up Prince. I was grateful that he finished a few moments later and slid off of me. I wrapped myself up in the cover and slid next to Prince until Nas decided to leave. Since I'd been living in this house, I could count the number of times on one hand that he stayed a whole night with us and tonight, I had no reason to think things would be any different. His speech was slurred when he decided to speak,

"Why… why you actin' like that, Ma? Why are you bein' like that to me, huh?"

"You're drunk, Nas. You shouldn't have even brought yo' ass over here if you was gon' be like this."

"Drunk? Shit, I had one… maybe three drinks and shit, how the fuck am I drunk?"

"You tell me. Yo' ass the one stumbling up the stairs and slurring all yo' words together."

He stood up, struggling to keep his balance, "you know what, you gon'... you gon' get enough of talkin' to me anyway. Like I'm some fuck boy or some shit."

"Then you need to stop actin like one, nigga."

"What?"

I flipped the covers off of me and stood right in front of him. Outside of my bra, I was completely naked as his attention shifted from my face down to my body. "Damn," he said, "are you gettin' thicker? Got-damn!" He reached out to try to touch my ass, but I smacked his hand away, "You need to go, nigga. You come in here actin' like that, and Prince is tryin' to sleep. Get the fuck out."

"This... this is my house! I pay the mortgage in this bitch, the fuck you mean get out? No, you get out!"

"Muthafucka, you ain't paid shit since me and Prince been in this house. I'm the one, nigga. Me, not you. Take yo' silly ass up outta here."

"Fuck you, Lyric. Fuck you."

"Yeah, fuck you too, muthafucka."

He turned and headed back down the stairs when suddenly I heard a crash. He got halfway down the stairs before he tipped over and fell the rest. I went over and stood at the top stair to check on him, "Nas! Nas, you alright!" He laughed, "Shiiiit, I'm good, Ma. I just tripped over a penny and shit." Moments later, Loc walked to the stairs and helped him up and just like that, the both of them were gone. I turned the lights off and snuggled back into the bed next to Prince. I still loved Nas; I loved him to shit, but Big Mama was right when I went to the grave earlier. I needed to get away from him somehow, but the problem with that was I wasn't sure if I wanted to. I think I was addicted to the danger aspect he brought into my life, and if that was cut out, I think I would have begun to feel sort of lost. Prince stretched out next to me as I patiently waited to see if he would wake up. He turned over and went back to sleep as I laid there, watching him sleep peacefully for the rest of the night.

Chapter 9

I sat in the visitor's room, waiting for him to come to the front. It all happened so quickly. Last night, he was drunk at the house and this morning, he was locked up. I got a call from Man-Man, letting me know what happened. It turned out that he got into a fight with some off-duty police officers after he left my house. He had two unregistered pistols on him and a few bags of coke so they arrested him on the spot. The gun and possession charges were serious in our city, so this wasn't something he could just post bail on and get on with his day. He finally came out into the room dressed in a dark green jumpsuit with his hands cuffed in front of him. He smiled when he saw me and they unloosened his cuffs so he could sit down and talk. I grabbed the phone as we looked at each other through the thick-plated glass that separated us.

"You aight?"

"I'm good, shit. Jail ain't shit to me, you know what I'm sayin'. I'll be out this bitch in a minute."

"How did you even get caught with that shit on you?"

"One of the muthafuckas had sticky fingers so I handled it and just forgot that it was on me. A lot of shit was going on that night, and it just slipped my mind."

"Damn, Nas. So now what?"

"Shit, I got my lawyers on it and them doin' what they can to get me out this muthafucka as quick as they can. Shit, I'm payin' them $150 an hour, so I know they better get this shit squared away for me or they gon' have another problem on they hand."

"Nas, you might wanna calm that shit down. You know they are listening."

"Fuck them!" he said out loud, causing the guards to focus their attention on him. The room went silent for a few moments before he spoke again,

"I'm runnin' shit in here anyway. Muthafuckas in here know me, so I'm Gucci, you know what I'm sayin'. This is why I'm King."

"Aight."

He looked at me through the glass as if he was struggling to say something. As his mind was moving one hundred miles a minute and he just didn't know how to get the words out.

"Say it, Nas."

He laughed, "I love when you do that shit. It's like you already know I got somethin' I need to say. But yo', I think you need to get out of the city for a while, you feel me? I believe it would be best for you and Prince."

"What? Why?"

I was surprised that he even said that, especially since Big Mama spoke through me at the graveyard. I guess God was real because this was the prayer I specifically sent to him but even though he gave me what I wanted, I still wasn't ready to accept it.,

"Why do we need to leave the city, Nas?"

"Because. We finally got some competition now. An OG nigga they call Blood. I don't even think I need to tell you why the call him that but shit, he doesn't fuck around."

"Is that supposed to scare me?"

"This ain't about you, Lyric," he said, a scowl appearing on his face, "This is about y'all. Us. This is about y'all being my weakness. If y'all is out of the city then the muthafucka can't do shit to me, but if y'all are here, then he got me to my knees if he gets his hands on y'all, you feel me? I can't risk that shit. Now, Man-man is—"

"Fuck that."

He paused, shooting daggers at me through his eyes.

"Lyric, this shit ain't up for discussion. I just got the drop that the nigga been watching us for a minute. He probably had something to do with that bitch almost getting murdered, but like I said, I am not takin' no chances. I need y'all gone until I can figure out how to handle this nigga."

"Fuck. That."

"Lyric!"

"Fuck that! I have never been the type of bitch to run from nobody, and you expect me to let some nigga run me and my family out my fuckin' city? Fuck that, Nas. You can keep that shit."

He was silent for a moment as he held the phone in his hand, peering back at me with enough venom foaming from his mouth to kill me with one bite. Suddenly, he slammed the phone onto the table, breaking the receiver and ripping the cord out of the wall. He yelled through the window, and I could barely hear him, but I knew what he was saying. "If something happens to my son cuz of you, then you gon' have to answer to me, bitch! You hear me!" he yelled as the guards came to restrain him. "You hear me! You betta hope and fuckin' pray that nothing happens to him!"

They drug him out of the room as I sat there with the phone still in my hand, thankful that the animal was caged for the time being. It was crazy how, almost immediately, everything was setting up for me to make my way out of the city and away from Nas but I still rejected it. It was a classic case of somebody drowning in the lake and being tossed a raft just to end up pushing the raft away. I couldn't explain it, but that's just how I was. I didn't want to get in the raft.

I drove to Big Mama's house when I left. I remembered Vinny telling me he had the day off so I wanted to go by there to see if anything was going on with Uncle Stew. When I pulled up, his car was in the driveway, and the front door was cracked open. He walked out moments later.

"What's good, Sis?"

I walked up to the porch and took my regular seat.

"Shit. I'm aight I guess."

"I heard yo' boy got knocked last night."

"Yeah. I just came from visiting him and shit."

"What he get locked up for?"

"Unregistered gun and a couple of bags of coke."

"Damn. That gun charge is about to fuck him over."

"Unless somebody else catches the charge for him. He said Man-Man was in there too, and I don't think he has a record, so I don't know."

"Shit, that would be the only thing he could do to get his ass out."

A few cars rode by blasting their music with the windows down. Summer was coming to an end, so everybody was out stunting and getting their last bit of shine out before the weather changed.

"Nas trying to get me to take Prince and move out of the city for a while."

"What? Why?"

"You heard about a nigga named Blood?"

"Ooh, yeah. Matter of fact, I did. Walter and nem' were telling me about some OG ass nigga from Baltimore that just moved here. Yeah."

He looked at me while I remained speechless, waiting for him to piece it all together himself.

"Oh shit! Hell yeah, then you should probably take Prince and get the fuck out of here, Lyric. Straight up."

As much as I didn't want to listen, they were right. That was the exact thing Mrs. Butler warned me about with Prince. He could end up being hurt because of my carelessness the same way Uncle Stew was. Vinny spoke up, "Come on, Lyric. This ain't just about you. I mean, if it was and you wanted to stay, then that's on you, but you can't think that way with Prince involved, you know what I'm sayin'? You just can't do that shit." I looked over to the streetlights as the darkness set in around them, causing them to flicker on, "Fuck. I know. I know, Vinny. That's all I keep hearing, *it ain't about you, it ain't about you.* I get it." He walked over and put his arm around me, saying, "it ain't forever. Just until some shit blow over. I mean, you and Nas got the city on lock so maybe y'all both can get away for a minute, you know? Shit. I wish I could; I need a vacation." My eyes lit up.

"Yo, so why don't you... why don't you come with us for a minute? I mean, any place we go, we're going to be driving. Shit, I'll pay for your plane ticket back here and shit. Come on, Vinny. Please? I just don't wanna go by myself."

"Aight, fam. Just let me check with my job and put in the vacation request. When are you trying to leave?"

"I guess as soon as possible."

"Aight then. I'll hit you up tomorrow and let you know whassup."

I reached over and hugged Vinny tight around his neck. It shocked him at first because I was never the type to do that. I couldn't remember a time that I had hugged him like this before, but he slowly lifted his arms up and embraced me back. Another car drove by with its music blasting, base vibrating everything around us. Seconds later, I saw children running down the block full speed as if they were chasing the car on foot. I was going to miss Milwaukee, and I didn't want to let it go, but I knew it was the best thing for us right now.

It took a few weeks for me to convince myself to go and get shit settled for the trip out of town. Every time I talked to Nas over the phone, he was telling me to get the fuck out of Milwaukee. "Yo, Lyric, I'm not fuckin' playin. Get yo' ass the fuck out this city, yo'. Straight up." After the first couple times, he sounded like a broken record, so I just started hanging up on him. He had been trying to get me to leave for a couple of weeks before I finally caved in. I decided to go back to Chicago and keep a low profile. I had enough money so I wouldn't have to work; it would be like a vacation for me. At this point, it felt like a fresh beginning for me. Like I didn't go there before and had to deal with being raped and robbed all at once. That was almost two years ago now and from what I could tell, I was over it. Vinny said that he was good to chill with me for a week or so, but that's all the time he had for vacation. One week was better than none, so that was good enough for me. I had all my bags packed at the house as Loc stood with me just for added security.

"Aight, Loc. I'm about to grab Prince and then I'll be back here."

"Let me go with you."

"Loc, I'm good. Niggas ain't did shit to me since I been driving through this city so what make you think something gon' happen now."

"I hear you, but Nas said—"

"Fuck Nas, I got this. You just chill right here and make sure nobody come through to try and take my shit, aight?"

"But—"

"Appreciate it, Loc."

I responded to him without giving him a chance to rebuttal and seconds later I was gone. The trip to Mrs. Butler's house went quicker than normal. It was usually about a 30-minute drive but for some reason, the majority of the lights on the main streets were green when I approached them. The weather was pretty cool for one of the final days of summer. The bus stops were full of people with somber, dejected looks on their faces while they waited for the city transit to come. I remembered those days as a teenager but most of the time, I was out there hanging with Junie and Vinny, cracking jokes and rapping to pass the time. I couldn't help but reminisce as I waited for the light ahead of me to turn green. I glanced out my rearview mirror and saw a black Navigator sitting a few cars behind me. I wasn't sure, but it seemed as if it had been following me for the past few minutes, making all the same turns I did but staying just a few cars behind me every time. The light finally turned green, and I pulled out into the intersection, keeping an eye on the black truck. Just then, it veered off to the left and made a turn. *I'm tripping*, I said to myself as I finally got to Mrs. Butler's house.

She had him bundled and ready to go as soon as I got there. She told me that there hadn't been any other incidents since the last time she was attacked, but Allen had gotten pistols for the both of them since that day, and she kept hers nearby at all times. They had even gotten one for Serena, but she was too afraid to use it. She almost passed out when they put in her hand; I laughed just remembering the story she told me about it. Prince smiled when he saw me and Mrs. Butler looked as if she was bittersweet about my decision,

"Baby, now you know I'm happy that you and Prince are getting out of this crazy city," she wiped a tear from her eye, "but just because I'm happy don't mean I can't be sad about the same thing."

"I know, Mama. I mean, you guys can visit anytime you—"

She cut me off, "Oh, you think we're not? We already planned to come out that way next weekend. I think Serena is going to go with us, too, but you know how she is. She plans to do something one second and the next; she backs out of it. I hate it when she does that."

I laughed, "Junie used to do the same thing, and it drove me crazy!"

"Girl, I don't see how you dealt with it."

There was an uncomfortable silence between us while we both reminisced on Junie as Prince laughed, swiping at some imaginary thing that was hanging in front of him.

"How are you doing with Nas? I mean, I know it's probably late for me to even talk to you about this but better late than never."

"It's tough at times, you know? I mean, because they are so much alike. At times, I thought Nas was a better fit for me because he was, um…" I searched for a way to say it that didn't imply his sexual nature, "a little more aggressive than Junie was, you know? We were a lot alike in that sense, but as I stay with him, going on two years now, I realize that being just alike is not what it should be. Now, I find myself thinking about Junie a little more, and it's torturing me because I know there is not a chance we will get back together. I just have this lookalike in front of me, and I don't think it's good enough."

"I understand, baby. I mean, your father and I are nothing alike at all. Nothing, but because of that, we work well together.

That's just life. Things never fit the way you think it should. It fits the way it wants to fit."

"Yeah, I know. Are you ok with not being close to your son?"

"It hurts a lot, you know. Especially when he came over here and sat in our front room, and I couldn't tell him. I couldn't hold him and call him *son*. I couldn't do any of that, and it hurt. It still hurts to this day, but I realize that he is a grown man and it's not something he is probably looking for. It's like I had to let him go but I never really got to hold him to begin with."

We sat in the front room for at least an hour, talking and deepening our relationship. She wasn't Big Mama, but if there were somebody that had to fill in the gap for her, Mrs. Butler would have undoubtedly been my choice. After we had spoken, I got up and took Prince outside, and we headed back to my house. It was around 6 pm when I stopped at a red light on Burleigh, a busy street on Milwaukee's north side. I glanced across the street at the Boys and Girls Club that sat on the corner, watching young boys playing basketball outside on the playground. I fantasized about that being Prince out there one day with his friends and realized that if I didn't make this move out of the city now, he might not get the opportunity. The light turned green, and I pulled out into the intersection when suddenly, another car slammed on its breaks, sliding across the intersection and smacking right into the front of my car. My airbag exploded into my face, knocking me backward into the seat. Everything was hazy for a moment as I heard Prince crying in the backseat. "Prince, you ok, baby?" I said, slowly coming back to consciousness. I finally got out the front seat, seeing some cars frozen around me as people ran up to my car to check on me. I pushed them away. "Back up; I gotta check on my baby," I said as I did my best to garner strength and push them off. His cries were interrupted by the yelling of the woman whose car smacked into me.

"Bitch, what the fuck is wrong with you?! Pullin out into the intersection like that! Bitch, you saw me coming! If you didn't, you should have!" I turned to look in her direction, squinting my eyes to get a better view of her. It took me a few moments to put it together but I when I did, it was almost as if my body went cold. Keyonna stood there just on the side of her car, her long blond hair tied up in a ponytail as she peered at me with her arms folded across her chest. "Keyonna?" I said as I leaned my weight on the hood of my car. She walked closer to me, whispering in my ear, "yeah bitch, it's me. You didn't think this shit was over, did you? Nah, fuck that. You couldn't have thought that." Police sirens went off in the background, and I could tell they were getting closer by the second. Just then, she smiled at my left at a passenger in another car. The sirens got louder as I struggled to get to the back of my car to check on Prince. I glanced inside of his car seat, but he was gone. My eyes bucked as I flung the door open, refusing to believe my eyes but there was nothing left. His diaper bag was still on the seat and the bottle he was sucking on had fallen to the floor. "My baby! Where the fuck is he!" I yelled, mustering the last bit of strength I had. I looked around the scene of the accident as I became disoriented until I eventually lost my balance and crashed into the pavement.

I saw people rushing up to me for help as the sirens became louder and louder. The last thing I saw was Prince's baby bottle on its side, his milk dripping slowly onto the pavement matching the tears that left my eyes. Moments later, I blacked out.

Chapter 10

I woke up in the hospital and immediately tried to jump out the bed, "My son!" I yelled at the top of my lungs, "Let me the fuck out of here; I gotta find my son!" The doctors rushed in, pushing me back down onto the bed as I fought them off.

"Get the fuck away from me! I need to find my son! My fuckin' son is missing! They took him! That bitch took him!"

"Ok, Ma'am, calm down. Just keep cool, ok? The authorities are on their way to help you."

"Fuck that! They don't need to help me; they need to find my son!"

"We're going to need to give her something to calm her down," the doctor said to the nurse as a few more of them came to try to restrain me. I threw my fists, connecting with a few of them and meeting the others with the bottom of my feet. Eventually, more of them came in and held me down as they stuck a needle in one of the tubes that were connected to my arm. Moments later, I calmed. My kicking and punching came to a silence and my eyes shut again. When I reopened them, my arms were tied to the bed and officers stood in front of me. I tried to yank myself free but it was to no avail, I wasn't going anywhere. The detective stood in front of me and said,

"Lyric Sutton, right?"

"Find my son."

"We will get to that, but we at least need to know who we are talking to."

"Find my fuckin' son or let me go so I can."

"Ma'am."

"Let me go!!!!!"

I yelled as I struggled to break my arms and legs free to throw more blows at them as the detective dropped his arms to his side and watched me struggle. The more I tried to break free, the more tired I became. Eventually, I just stopped, still breathing hard with a rage that would have killed somebody if I had the chance. "Are you done?" he asked sarcastically as I gathered a mouthful of spit and hurled it at him. He watched it connect with his suit coat as another officer walked to my bed, his face reddened, ready to pay me back some way. The detective put his hand on the officer's chest, keeping him from getting any closer to me. His demeanor was calm even though a mouthful of my saliva just splattered right on his chest. He took out a napkin and wiped his vest off, then tossed the napkin inside the trash can. His brown skin was as smooth as pudding, his mustache was thin, and his beard was a trimmed five-o'clock shadow. If I had to guess, he would have been a movie star before I pegged him as a detective. He was gorgeous, but I quickly went back to the reason I spat at him in the first place,

"I need to find my son. Please! Let me go!"

I yanked harder just to have the same outcome. The detective folded his arms across his chest as he spoke to the rogue officer, "You don't do anything to a woman like this. This is a mother who just lost her son, and if she wants to take her anger out on you, you let her. If she is trying to curse you out and yell, you take it. As long as she is not doing anything to threaten your life, you let her vent. That is your fucking duty. To protect and serve," he said to the officer just beyond him. I didn't know if it was a good cop, bad cop act, but if it was I believed him. Suddenly, I calmed down to a state of mind that he could communicate with rationally. He turned towards me,

"Your name?"

I huffed, "Lyric Sutton."

"Do you know who it was that hit your car?"

I knew exactly who she was. She was the girlfriend of Big Tuck, the drug dealer I extracted revenge on for killing Junie. She was the woman I sometimes fucked just to get close enough to Big Tuck for me to kill him. She was the chick that Nas wanted to kill and that I foolishly told him not to spare her life. Yeah, I knew exactly who she was.

"No."

"Really?" the detective walked closer to me, "because she may have something to do with your son's disappearance. Are you sure you don't know who she is?"

"I'm sure. I don't know her. Never seen her before until she smacked into my car with hers. Can't you run the plates or something?"

"The car had no plates. It was a stolen vehicle that somehow ended up here from Waukegan, IL. Do you know anybody down there?"

"No, I don't."

"Do you know of anybody who didn't like you? Enemies?"

"Sir, I have a bunch of those. All I remember is getting into an accident and then all of a sudden my fuckin' son is gone. That's all I got for you now if you can get me the fuck out of here so I can find my son, I would appreciate that."

"We're out looking for him now. Checking with witnesses and all of that but something tells me that you know more than what you're telling me."

"Something tells me that y'all need to fuckin' let me go if I'm not being arrested. This is some violation; y'all can't just keep me here like a fuckin' prisoner. Am I being arrested?"

"No."

"Then get these fuckin' doctors in here and tell them to cut me fuckin' loose to I can find my mutha fuckin' son! The shit is not that hard to fuckin' understand! Let me the fuck go!"

He lowered his notebook and turned to the other officers and seconds later, they all left the room, and the doctors came in right after. They stood just in front of me, explaining the plethora of injuries I had and doing their best to convince me to keep myself in the hospital but nothing, not even God Himself, would be able to keep me in this place while my son was missing. Time was passing rapidly, and I knew I had to make a move before it was too late. Keyonna was the only lead I had to go with, and I was coming straight for her like a heat-seeking missile.

I called Vinny as soon as they left so I could get a ride from him. I didn't want to call Loc because then word would get back to Nas, and I knew all hell would break loose. He had been trying to get me to move for the past few weeks and the fact that I stalled wouldn't do anything but piss him off. Not just because I stayed longer than I should have but the fact that since I did, Prince got kidnapped. I didn't even want him to know about it and in a perfect world, I would find Prince and get him back home before he or anybody else noticed.

It was around 9:30 pm when Vinny showed up in a panic. "Fuck, Lyric! They took Prince?!" he said as soon as I jumped into the car. "Yeah, I need to get on this shit. Take me to Big Tuck's old crib. I need to look there first." He paused as he looked at me in disbelief, "Big Tuck old spot? It's fuckin' wild over there now, Lyric. Like—," I cut him off, "Listen, I don't have time to hear that shit! Either take me over there or drop yo' ass off at home and I'll take my fuckin' self. Either way, I'm there!"

He leaned forward, momentarily looking around and then accelerated. I leaned back in my seat with nothing but anger and worried dripping from my mind. *What if they are hurting him right now*, I thought to myself, *I'ma fucking kill that bitch. I swear on everything I love that bitch is dead on sight.* We eventually pulled up to Big Tuck's old crib, parking just a few houses away. A few crackheads walked around the neighborhood aimlessly as if they were searching for something that could be sold. I sat and observed Big Tuck's house, looking for any sign of life inside. The front windows were broken, and tall blades of grass seemed to swallow the porch steps whole. The grass in front of the house looked as if it hadn't been cut in a few months. I could tell Vinny was nervous; I saw him always checking his side and rearview mirrors every few seconds. That was cool with me though because out here, you could never be too careful. Seconds later, there was a knock on our window, and Vinny damn near shit his pants, "What! What the fuck?" he said, cracking his window. A fiend stood just on the other side of the car.

"Any of y'all wanna buy a radio? It's good quality. Got the AM and FM stations and it even has an ala—"

"Bruh, get the fuck away from my car. Don't nobody wanna buy no fuckin' radio with a cassette player on the front? Who the fuck have tapes anymore? Get the fuck out of here! Scarin' the shit out of me like that."

He rolled his window back up as we watched the crackhead walk away, struggling to stay in a straight line. That is all that was out here these days. I thought about the last time I came here with Junie. We were in the exact some spot I was parked in right now, and no fiends were walking around like there was right now. Tuck kept those niggas away from his spot because they were known to steal any and everything around the area. You could tell he was gone now, but he deserved it and technically, you could say he brought it on himself. If he never had Junie murdered, he might still be running the city right now. Vinny broke me out of my daydream,

"So, what… what do you know about the kidnapping right now?"

I peered at the house while I was ducked down in the passenger's seat, "All I know is Keyonna was the last person I saw before I realized my son was missing. She's the one who smacked into my car and shit."

"Keyonna? The chick that used to fuck with Tuck?"

"Yeah, that's her. I knew I should've let Nas kill that bitch when he had the chance."

"Shit, we in the wrong spot then. Keyonna lives on the south side."

"How you know?"

"I just saw her over there the other day, driving around in a white BMW."

"How you know her?"

"Everybody in Milwaukee knows that chick, especially before Tuck got popped. She was everywhere, you know what I'm sayin'. Hood famous and shit."

"Let's go over there then, shit, this muthafucka look dead as a bitch."

Just as Vinny pulled off, a light inside Tuck's house flickered on, "Wait, stop," I said to him as he smashed on the brakes. "What is it?" I pointed to the house, "That right there is what it is." He noticed the light that was just switched on then he looked back towards me.

"Now what?"

"Shit, I'm gonna go check it out. Back up and park right there again. I'ma be right back."

Vinny parked the car as I crept out of the passenger's seat. I didn't have a pistol on me or anything, and I didn't even realize it until I got halfway to the house, but I didn't care. The anger I felt right now was enough for me to kill someone with my bare hands. All I cared about was Prince and if that meant putting myself in danger just so I could get him back, then so be it. I walked casually to the side of the house, doing my best to blend in with the few bodies that were roaming around the neighborhood. It didn't take long for me to make it to the side of the house. The window was too high up for me to peek inside, so I crept around the back, stepping over beer cans and trash that was littered all over the yard.

The back yard was huge, and there was a shed not far from the house. I could only imagine the number of deaths and tortures that went on inside of there while Tuck was living. The stench hit my nose as soon as I stepped into the yard. It could have been my imagination but then again, so much could have happened back here that the smell just lingered, no matter how long ago everything happened. I crept up to the back door and put my hand on it as it slowly moved it open with the slightest touch. I looked all around me before I stepped inside, still crouched like a thief. The house inside seemed to be abandoned. Drawers were pulled out of their places and flipped over onto the ground. Other than that, the kitchen was empty. The tiles on the floor had begun to bulge in particular places, and the walls were a dingy, off-white color. I crept through the mess and went into the hallway, coming closer and closer to the light that flickered on. I heard a movement, sounding as if it was a spoon stirring inside of pot. I crept closer until I got to the room and that's when I saw him. He was stretched out on the floor with his head resting against the wall. His eyes were rolled to the back of his head as I looked down at his arm. The string was tied around it with a syringe lying on the floor right next to him. I looked over at another man as he continued stirring the pot, not even recognizing that I was there.

"What the fuck did you do to him!?" I yelled, running towards Uncle Stew as he lay on the ground, lifeless. The man jumped, knocking the pot of water over that was boiling on top of a warmer. Moments later, he got up and jumped out the window, but I didn't care about him. I untied the string from Uncle Stew's arm and slapped him in the face, trying to wake him from his sleep.

"Uncle Stew! Uncle Stew! Come on, man please, Uncle Stew!"

The more I yelled and smacked him in the face, I realized that it was anger coming out of me. I was slapping him with more and more force each time but he never even budged. He just took the punishment as the whites of his eyes continued to be the only thing I saw. It was at that moment that I knew he was gone. I stopped yelling and grabbed him around his neck, pulling him closer to me as the tears rolled out of my eyes. His body was still warm and because of that; I knew he overdosed not too long ago. As I peered at him, I saw my Mama's face appear on his body, and I froze. It was horrifying to see her dead in my arms, and before it became too much to bear, I heard another person come into the room, and I spun around. Vinny stood there with a horrified look on his face, not knowing what to say. As he inched closer to us, he bent down and placed his hand on my back, "Yo, Lyric. Let's go. Come on." I turned back to Uncle Stew, and his face had reappeared on his body.

I held him a bit longer as I cried, rocking back and forth with him in my arms. I know Big Mama said that I shouldn't blame myself for this, but I couldn't see it any other way. He was dead and if I hadn't foolishly left that crack inside Big Mama's house, he might not have been dead right now. To think that he ended up dying the same way my mama did was something I would never forget. Vinny finally pulled me away from Uncle Stew and helped me out of the crack house, walking with his arm around me until we got to the car. As he drove away, I had to do my best to collect myself. I knew the last time I saw Uncle Stew would probably be the last time I would see him alive. I just never expected to see him dead.

I refused to let Vinny take me home, and we headed to the south side where he last saw Keyonna. That side of the city was full of Puerto Ricans and Mexicans, and I hadn't spent much time over there at all to know anything about it. But Vinny? He knew this side well, and mainly it was because most of the chicks he talked to were either Puerto Rican or Mexican. It was 11:30 pm when we pulled into a gas station on 24th and Chambers. We were just on the outskirts of the hood, and I didn't want to go any further without having a pistol or anything on me. We sat at the same gas station he saw her at for a little while hoping that, by chance, she would pop up. She never did. Vinny looked over at me, "Lyric, you wanna roll? Let's look again tomorrow, aight? I'll take the day off." I nodded my head, and we left. "He's gonna be aight, Lyric. I promise. We will find my nephew and everything will be back to normal." As we drove away from the South Side, I got a text message, *Hey, baby. I think I've found what you're looking for.* I clicked on the photo and up came a picture of Prince, still wrapped in his baby blanket and sound asleep inside of another car seat. Another text message came through right after, *I bet it's fucked up to see somebody take something away from you that you loved. Look, we don't want to hurt him, but if you want to see this little nigga again, I suggest you give us what we want. Aight? Bye, baby.*

I called the number right after I read the text but the phone was disconnected. I hung up and called back again, getting the same response. "Fuck!" I yelled out, causing Vinny to swerve as he drove,

"What, Lyric?! What!?"

"That bitch got Prince!" I said, passing him the phone.

He looked at it in horror and tossed it back to me, his eyes focused intensely on the road and not saying a word to me. I cried again, punching the dashboard until my fists throbbed. They had me in a choke hold, and I would probably die trying to get out of it.

Chapter 11

I saw him out the corner of my eyes as I crept down a long, narrow hall. He was being rocked in the arms of somebody I had seen before, but I couldn't quite put the name on his face. I looked around to make sure nobody spotted me and then inched closer to him. He looked as if he didn't have a care in the world as he smiled in the man's arms. As I crept closer, his face began to become clearer. Junie sat, holding Prince in his arms with the biggest smile on his face. I stood up when I got to the end of the long hallway, confused by what I was seeing.

"Junie?"

He looked towards me, "Whassup, Lyric. Prince just got here. I was wondering when you were coming."

Suddenly, the hall that I stood in turned into a bright white glow. I looked down, and it seemed as though I was walking on air but none of that even bothered me, I was focused on Prince. Walking towards him, I held my arms out to receive him from Junie, but Prince didn't budge. He didn't even reach back for me; his tiny hands clenched onto Junie's shirt tighter as he made himself more comfortable in his arms.

"I guess he doesn't want to go with you," Junie said, flashing his new newly acquired, dimple-laced smile.

"I don't know why," I said, then turning towards Prince, "Hey baby, its mama. You don't want to come with Mama?"

It seemed as though he looked right through me and turned back to Junie. I looked away, focusing on where I was. *This had to be a dream*, I said to myself, *this is all a dream*. Suddenly, Big Mama walked from out of nowhere and came to

Junie and Prince. She put her arms around both of them and leaned in to kiss them on their cheeks.

"Big Mama?" I said, questioning her actions, "you don't see me?"

"Oh, Lyric? I… I just wasn't expecting you, that's all. Give your Grandma a hug."

She walked over to me and squeezed me around my neck, but it all felt fake. It was like I saw these loved ones but I didn't feel their spirits like I usually did before. They were so distant from me even though they were right in the same room. I turned towards Junie as blood began dripping from his forehead but even with that, he kept smiling. The blood slowly dripped from his head and splashed onto Prince. I ran towards them, but Big Mama held me back. "Big Mama, let me go! Something is happening to them! I have to—" and the moment I spun around, Big Mama's face changed before my eyes. She was no longer the young-looking, beautiful grandmother I had grown to know. Her skin seemed to cling to her body like Saran wrap and her weight dropped from her body drastically making her appear to look like a skeleton. I jerked away from her, and she had a look of sadness on her face. I spun back around to Prince and Junie only to notice that Junie had completely tilted his head back in the recliner and was no longer breathing. Prince was somehow still in his arms with Junie's blood stained on his face. I reached towards Prince, grabbing him into my arms and squeezing him tight. His baby coo's stopped almost immediately when I grabbed him, so I held him to my face only to notice that he wasn't breathing. "No, no! Prince!" I yelled as I laid him on the ground and snatched his clothing off to see if he was injured in some way. Moments later, Big Mama put her delicate hand on my shoulder, "It doesn't have to be this way," she said in a soft, brittle voice. I looked back at Prince, and he still didn't move, so I grabbed a hold of him to try to wake him up as Junie's blood was still stained on him.

"Prince! Prince! Baby, please wake up! Mama is sorry, Mama is so sorry!"

"Lyric?"

Vinny looked at me as he sat on the side of my bed with a cold towel in his hand. I had the sides of his arms clamped in my hands, breathing slowly as I scanned the room for a dose of reality. He waited for me to say something as I relaxed and laid back down on the bed,

"I... I just had the craziest dream, Vinny. I don't even know what to make of it."

"I understand, you don't have to explain nothing to me, Lyric."

"What time is it?"

"It's about 8 o'clock."

Suddenly, I remembered what I was doing last night and jumped out of bed. I was still in the same clothes I wore yesterday.

"Prince! We have to find Prince, Vinny! Shit! It's been a whole night! Why did you fuckin' let me sleep the whole night!? Anything could happen to him!"

He watched me frantically run around my room, looking for my shoes, "My bad, Lyric. I knew you needed some rest, though."

"Fuck my rest; I need to find Prince!"

My shoes were playing the vilest game of hide-n-seek at the worse moment. Vinny tried to get my attention, but his words fell on deaf ears as I ran out to the front room. My shoes were right by the front door of the house, and I moved to put them on.

"Lyric, um. It's some dudes outside for you."

I immediately stopped what I was doing, "Some dudes?"

"Yeah. They came in here lookin' for you, but when I asked them to wait outside because Big Mama was sick and I didn't want her to wake up, they left and stood in the driveway by their truck."

I ran to the window and peeked outside. Loc and two other men stood by the car for an escort service waiting for me to come outside. I shook my head, knowing what they were here for. Somehow, they found out about Prince, and they were taking me to see Nas. That was the last place I wanted to go. I thought about escaping through the back door, but that would cause me to have to travel through the city on the bus since they had blocked Vinny's car in the driveway. I couldn't get around like that today, not at all. I took a deep breath and put my hand on the door as Vinny grabbed me,

"Lyric, you sure you want to go with them?"

"I don't have a choice, Vinny. Besides, I can find Prince quicker if they are helping me."

"Or maybe Nas will have them kill you for letting Prince get kidnapped."

I paused before I twisted the handle on the door, "If that's the case, then so be it. At this point, I fuckin' deserve it."

"I'ma find him, Lyric," he said as I walked outside. Loc stood up and opened the back door of the car as I got in. Not a word was spoken between us as we backed out of the driveway and headed to Nas's prison just on the outskirts of the city. I couldn't imagine what was about to happen to me because of Prince's kidnapping but whatever it was, I was going to take it head on.

I sat on my side of the double-plated glass waiting for him to show up. The other inmates walked past me, making as little eye contact as they could. They didn't want to be the one caught looking at Nas's bitch; he marked his territory as soon as I came on my first visit. Finally, Nas walked outside, and when he put his eyes on me, he tapped the guard on the shoulder and walked back out. Moments later, a guard came behind me and got my attention, "Miss, please walk with me." I got up and followed him out of the room as he led me down a long corridor and into another room that didn't have any glass to keep Nas away from me. It was empty; there were only two chairs and one long table in the room that looked as if it was designed for one-on-one visits. I sat down in the chair as the guard that walked me over left me in there alone. I looked into the corners and scanned the walls for cameras, but there were none. I was going to be alone in the room with Nas with no security, and that scared the shit out of me.

He finally walked into the room. His chest poked through his shirt, and his arms seemed to have gotten a lot bigger since the last time I saw him. He flashed that dangerous smile at me as he walked towards me. I didn't know how to react because I wasn't sure how much he knew. He reached his arms out towards me, "Damn, what a nigga gotta do to get a hug from his bitch?" Nervously, I got up and put my arms around him, preparing to defend myself at any moment. To my surprise, he let me go but not before he ran his hands across my ass. Right after that, he pulled his pants down and sat in the chair. His dick shot up in the air as he motioned with his finger to come to him. I looked back at the door,

"What about the guards? What if they come in and—"

"Bitch, fuck them guards. I run this Muthafuckin' prison. They on my watch, now bring yo' ass over here and put yo' mouth on this dick."

I didn't know what was going on and for the moment, it appeared that he may not have known about Prince. I used that to my advantage and tried to keep the subject as far away from Prince as I could as I came over and slid my tongue up and down his penis. I licked the middle and slowly went to the top as I carefully observed him in the process. He was looking down at me, the same frightening smile he had when I came in never left his face as I bobbed up and down on his dick. I sucked on the tip of it and stroked it slowly with my hand before I put it all back in my mouth, still watching his actions. I wanted to put him so far in a state of pleasure that thoughts of Prince wouldn't even cross his mind. I put it all the way in my throat and came up, cum dripping from my mouth as he nodded his head. "That's my bitch right there," he said, shoving my head back down on him. When I came up the next time, even more cum dripped from my mouth as he ripped my pants off and turned me around. He fucked me so hard that I screamed. I saw the guard look into the room at us, but he just turned back around after he saw what was going on. I was expecting him to come in, but the door never opened as Nas put his dick deep inside of me, pulling my hair and smacking my ass so hard that I could feel the sting even seconds after he made contact with my skin. He only fucked rough for a few minutes before I felt his warm cum shoot inside of me. After he was done, he pulled his pants up and sat back down, "Aight bitch, take a seat."

I turned around to look at him, noticing he was different. Although I willingly had sex with him, I almost felt as bad as I did when I was raped at the strip club in Chicago. His disrespect for me was so similar to the disrespect I felt that night. Up and to this point, he'd never called me a bitch unless he was saying I was his bitch. He had never fucked me to the point that I had enough pain that I was almost ready to tell him to stop. He'd never treated me like I was just a worthless crack whore until now and that's when it dawned on me. He knew about Prince; he had to. I pulled up my pants, squeezing my ass over my jeans, and walked back over to my seat. The cum around my mouth had dried, and there was nothing to wipe it off with,

"Nas, can you get me a napkin or something?"

"I'll get it later."

We sat silently, staring back and forth at each other. His smile faded, and now, he looked at me with a bit of aggression. As time passed, the silence in the room became deafening, so I finally spoke up,

"You know when are you are gettin' out now?"

He sucked his teeth, "I'll get out when I'm out."

The guard coughed outside in the midst of the silence that floated in-between us,

"Nas, what the fuck you call me down here for if you just wanted to look at me like a fuckin' dumb ass."

I couldn't let off that I was nervous or afraid of him right now. The whole time we'd been together, I'd talk shit to him. I'd call him out his name and tell him how things were. I couldn't just switch my behavior right now and act like a scared little bitch. I knew who I was, and I wasn't going to let my situation change that. Not anymore. The venomous smile reappeared,

"So, you're going to sit there and not say shit about it?"

"Shit about what, nigga? Damn. I don't have time for these games, Nas. Open yo' mouth and say it. You're a grown ass man, stop actin' like a fuckin' little kid."

He laughed, "A little kid, huh? Funny you mention that. Lyric, where is Prince? Why didn't you bring him to see me?"

"Prince is at Mrs. Butler's house; you know he is over there during the day."

"Oh. You sure he's there?"

"Yeah. He goes there every day. What the fuck?"

"Because, from my understanding, Mrs. Butler has a lot on her plate right now. I mean, now that she has to bury her husband and shit, I would just assume that she didn't have time to keep an eye on my boy."

The expression on my face changed immediately as I thought back to Mrs. Butler. Prince hadn't been over there since last night, and I hadn't heard from her this morning when I was supposed to bring Prince over. My hands began to shake,

"Nas, the fuck you talking about?"

"I'm talking about Prince. Now, are you going to keep lying to me or do I have to beat the SHIT out of you for you to tell me where my son is?"

"Fuck this shit," I said as I stood up and headed for the door.

I heard his chair move, and seconds later, I felt his hand clutching my shoulder as he threw me back into the table. My back slammed against the side of it as my weight caused the table to flip over. I laid on the ground, writhing in pain as he stood over me, yanking me up by my hair,

"Now, I'm going to ask you one more time. Where the FUCK is my son?" he asked, gripping a handful of my hair.

I took my fingers and dug them into his eyes as he yelled and pushed me back into the ground, "You fuckin' bitch!" he said as I fell into the wall. He rubbed his eyes as I picked up one of the chairs and smacked him across the back with it. He fell to his knees as I ran to the door but it was locked from the outside. The guard turned to look at me as I banged on the door for help but he twisted back around and used his back to cover the small window. I spun around just in time to see Nas throw a punch at me. It connected right on the side of my cheek as I fell backward again and struggled to get away. He watched me run from him like a gazelle fleeing from a lion as he snatched his shirt off, exposing the muscles that rippled throughout his body.

"All I wanna know is where my fuckin' son is, Lyric. That's all I want to know. You tell me that shit and you can walk out of here."

I kept as much space between us as I could, "I don't fuckin' know, Nas, aight? Damn!" I started to tear up, "I got into an accident yesterday and next thing I knew, somebody took him out the car."

"An accident? You mean someone crashed into you almost a month after I told yo' ass to get the fuck out of the city? Is that what you're talkin' about, Lyric?"

He asked as he continued to approach me. I stopped running and stood against a wall, waiting for him to come near me. I knew a punch that almost anybody couldn't stand was a punch straight to the nose. As he walked towards me, I stood with one foot behind the other and right when he got within an arm's reach I swung with everything I had in me. I connected right with his nose, but it didn't do anything but turn his head to the side. He slowly looked back at me as blood trickled out his nostrils and over his mouth. "Bitch, that's all you got?" he said as he smacked me across the face and threw me to the other side of the room. I flew into the door as I heard a voice outside, "Hey, what's going on in there? Step aside!" Moments later, another guard came in and looked at me in horror, then turned and called for help on his radio. As soon as he sent the distress signal, Nas smacked the receiver out his hand and beat the guard relentlessly. The blood from his face splattered everywhere as the other guard finally came in, "Nas, Nas, stop! You're going to kill him! You're going to kill him!" Nas pushed the guard away from him and kept striking the first guard that came into the room. I put my hand over my face, imagining that the person who was getting beat could have been me if he hadn't come in.

The heartless, cold killer in Nas was out and at this point, I figured it was there to stay. There was no longer a balancing act between his softness and the hardcore thug that was inside of him. Seconds later, the room filled with guards and they had tased Nas and kicked him off the guard. He flexed, doing as much as he could to take in the shocks. His veins poked through his chest and his arms as he gritted his teeth, "You're dead!" he said, forcing the words out of his mouth. "Dead!" and with that, he passed out. Two of the guards that came in helped the officer that was beaten senseless; the other came to me to check on my wounds. "I'm sorry," he said, "I don't know how this ever could have happened." The guard that watched everything from beyond the door stood in the room as I was helped up. I snatched the baton off one of the guards and threw it at him, but he blocked it with his forearms, "that muthafucka just stayed there and watched from outside the room! He didn't do shit when he saw Nas beatin' my ass! He just let it happen! Fuck you! Fuck you!" I yelled as the other guard picked me up and carried me out the room. If I could have gotten a hold to one of their guns, I would have ended it right there. Thank God I couldn't though, I knew that Prince was still out there waiting for his Mommy to find him.

When I got outside, Loc was standing by the car with his arms folded across his chest. I paused, looking to the left and right at the other two men, not knowing what to expect. Loc walked towards me. "Lyric, let's go. I'm not going to hurt you. I want to help you find Prince," he said calmly as he reached for my hand. I yanked back, "Fuck that. You on Nas' payroll so I know what you're trying to do." He removed his extended hand as he stood in front of me, towering above like a building. After he had looked back at the other two men, he made a motion with his hand. They all got in the car, and he turned back to me, "Listen, you can trust me, or you can go off on your own. Either way, both of our jobs are to find Prince. I'm going to walk to this truck, though, and if you want a ride somewhere, then I suggest you come with us. Otherwise, you can sit here and wait for somebody else to get you."

He walked away from me as I weighed my options. There was no telling when I would be able to get a ride from out here back to the city and in the meantime, Prince would still be out there somewhere. I swallowed my anxiety and went with Loc to the truck. He held the back door open for me as I got in and he scooted in behind me.

The ride back to Milwaukee was excruciating. I called Mrs. Butler a few times, but the phone kept going to voicemail. I didn't know if Nas was serious about what happened to Mr. Butler but the more and more I called them with no response, the more I believed that he wasn't bluffing. I glanced at Loc, "What happened to Mr. Butler?" He didn't say a word back to me. He kept his gaze straight forward as the truck rode smoothly over the freeway pavement. His silence wasn't enough for me to jump to any conclusions because he wasn't one to talk much. I was surprised he said as much as he did when he approached me outside just a few moments ago. Before I knew it, we were back at my house. I peered at Loc for a second before I reached for the door handle. He grabbed me by my arm and held a pistol right to my head. My eyes widened as my heartbeat felt like it jumped into my throat. Suddenly, he turned the pistol around and handed it to me, tossing me a few clips as soon as I gripped the gun with my hand. I popped open the chamber; it was empty. "Thanks, Loc," I said as I got out the car, "and check the south side for Prince. That's where I'm going. That's where I think he is." He left before I could get to the sidewalk. I didn't understand his kindness, especially after Nas just beat me up and threatened to kill me when I was in the prison room with him. I watched the truck until it disappeared around the corner. The block was quiet. It was almost 1 pm, so I knew all the bad ass little kids were still in school by now. Vinny's car was parked in the driveway when I got home, but inside, he was nowhere to be found. I texted him,

Vinny, I'm back at the crib. Where are you at?

I'm at work. I left my ride there so you could use it. I got my nigga car right now, though, and as soon as I leave here, I'm going to the southside.

Aight. I'll be over there with you.

I jumped in Vinny's car and headed to Mrs. Butler's house. I had to knock a few times before Serena came to the door with bloodshot eyes. I feared the worst when I saw her expression. She opened the screen door and hugged me tight as I embraced her back. She was still crying, and I didn't know how long she had been.

"Serena, what's wrong?"

She sniffled, "They killed Daddy! They killed him!"

"Who, Serena? Who!?"

"I don't know! He never came back home last night, and Mama went to look for him this morning. He was found dead right in his car! They didn't even take nothing, Lyric! It was just a murder! Cold-blooded murder for no fucking reason!"

She threw her arms back around me as she cried inconsolably. She didn't know the reason, but I did. I remembered Nas mentioning a while back that he was only in prison on some possession and illegal firearms charges. He said that if they found out about the murder charge, he had no chance of getting out. Killing Mr. Butler had to be some warning for Stacey, even though she had no intentions of telling anybody in the first place. Too much was going on for me to process. From Prince's abduction to finding Uncle Stew dead in a crack house, and now finding out about Mr. Butler's murder. Too much shit was happening at once, and it felt as though I was going to faint under the weight of it all.

"Where is Mom, Serena?"

"She's down at the police station giving her statement. I didn't want to go, I just... I don't know, I honestly just don't know what to do right now, Lyric. First, Junie gets murdered, and now a couple of years later, Daddy is gone," her eyes kept exploding with tears, "who is next, Lyric? I just want to get the fuck out of this city! I just want to leave!"

I put my arms around her again, and I hated to leave her, but I had to find Prince. I had to get going before he ended up dead because of something I did to Big Tuck. People around me were dropping like flies, and I was the common denominator. I was the primary link between them all and I didn't want anybody else dead because of me. Times like these are when I fantasized about the rap game again. What my life would have been like if I didn't put it all down and follow Nas throughout this city. Maybe I would be on the Billboard top 20, chilling in Brooklyn, New York—the city that Junie and I had planned to move to once we got enough money. The life that I lived in an alternate universe would have been much better than the one I thought I wanted to live here.

I did my best to calm Serena down and told her to grab a hold of the pistol that Dad bought her just in case. She shook her head vehemently, "Fuck that, Lyric! A gun is what killed Dad and Junie! Fuck those things, Lyric! I just want to get the fuck out of here!" It hurt me to leave her, but I made sure she locked the door behind me when I left to head to the south side. I had an idea of where Keyonna was staying. It was deep in the hood over there, though, in the midst of some Puerto Rican gangs. None of that fazed me, though, especially when I was on a mission to get to Prince. The worst thing you can do is cross a mama bear while she is in a rage to defend her cubs. I loaded a fresh clip into my pistol and from that point on, I had tunnel vision all the way to the south side. I got a text from Vinny,

Lyric, I see her. I see her right now! She is on 42nd and Vilet! That's where her house is! I lied and said I was at work because I knew you would be mad that I went looking without you, but hurry up!

I threw my phone down and accelerated on the gas as much as I could. I wasn't going to stop for anything or anybody until I got to where I was going.

Chapter 12

      I pulled into the neighborhood on 42nd Street and texted Vinny. *I'm here, where you at?* A few moments later, I got his response, *I'm down towards the end of the block in a black Monte Carlo. These SA's are lookin' at me funny though so I'm about to pull off. Meet me at that gas station we went to yesterday.* I saw his car pull out his parking spot just a few moments later, and as I got to the house he pointed out, I crept slowly, watching for entry points and any other information I could use to make the break-in easier. I took a right instead of following Vinny and went through the alley to check out the back. The yard was small, and there was one door that went to the back of the house. To the left, there was a window, and it was cracked open just enough that I figured I could slide through it. Small, narrow spaces separated the houses on each side, and I knew that I could shimmy through them to get from the front to the back if I had to. From what I could see, there was no security back there, but that could all change in a matter of moments. Eventually, I made my way down the alley, and I met him back at the gas station. He got out the car; anxiety kept him from staying still and he said,

"I saw her, Lyric. I saw her. She got out the ride and went right into the house. The thing is, them SA's you saw on the corner? She knows them, and they were hanging around her crib like fuckin' months to a flame. I don't know if Prince is in there or whatever but shit, I'm willing to bet he is."

"Fuck. I think I'ma have to call Loc, Vinny. I think I'ma have to."

"Aight, bet."

He didn't know what just happened to me when I went to the prison to visit Nas, but I couldn't chance going up in there alone with Vinny. As far as I knew, Vinny had never even held a gun, let alone shot one. The phone rang a few times before he picked up. He didn't say anything when he got on the phone; it was just his personality. He always lived to make sure he had the upper hand in everything and that's why Nas had him as one of his leading men.

"Loc, I think I found Prince. He's over here on the south side. 42nd and Vilet, you know what I'm sayin'? It's a bunch of SA's out here though so I can't go in there by myself. Can you help me? Please?"

There was silence on the phone. I couldn't tell what was going through his head at the moment and honestly, I never could. He was such an enigma that I could never get a good read on him. "Please, Loc. I'm begging you. Look, I know shit about me and Nas is fucked right now, but this is for our boy. This is for Prince, aight? Just help me this time and after I know he is safe, y'all can do whatever the fuck y'all need to do to me. I just need to get my son safe, Loc. Please man, I'm begging you." Vinny stood nearby listening to our conversation, but I was too focused on listening to Loc to even pay attention to him. "Aight. We on the way."

He hung up right after that as it felt like a load of bricks lifted off my shoulders. I turned to look at Vinny as he stood by my door, waiting for an explanation. "Whassup with you and Nas, Lyric?" I slipped my phone in my pocket and glanced away from him. A few teens walked from outside the gas station with their pants sagging and squeezing their legs at the same time. Their purple shirts were fitted tight over their chests as they walked, laughing out loud at what one of them said. Another car pulled into the gas station and stopped at the pump, waving the two boys over to their vehicle. They shook hands with the driver and kept walking. A drug transaction in motion so fluid that the naked, untrained eye wouldn't have been able to point it out. The man inside the car looked in our direction for a moment and then sped away from the pump. "Nothin, Vinny. We just got into some shit, that's all," I said as I kept my eyes away from him.

"Lyric, for real, whassup? You tellin' them that they can do whatever to you after y'all get Prince? What the fuck is that? You know what I'm sayin'? Like, what type of shit is between y'all?"

"Damn, Vinny, just leave it the fuck alone. It doesn't have shit to do with you, aight? Just let it be."

"Let it be? You talkin' about Prince, though. Shit, if something happens to you then—"

"Then he will still be aight! Shit! You actin' like a bitch right now, damn! I told you everything was straight, now just chill!"

I could tell he was hurt by how I just came at him. He turned around and walked back to his car. "Whatever, Lyric," he said on his way. That was my brother, but I didn't want him to get in-between anything that was going to happen after we got Prince. This was my problem and I'd already gotten enough people hurt and even killed at this point, I didn't need another death weighing on my conscious. I sat back down in my car, and as I waited for Loc, I texted Vinny, *Yo, why don't you just go ahead and get back to the crib. I'll meet you there.* I looked over at him as he read the text. He peered back at me as he shook his head and sent back another text, *Nigga, if it weren't for me, you wouldn't even know where Prince was, and now you are telling me to go home like I'm a pussy ass nigga or something? I came here to find Prince, so that's what I'ma do.* I thought it was crazy that we were only about 10 feet away from each other, but yet, we were sending text messages to each other like we were in another state. *"This is not you, Vinny. This not even who you are. I don't need you gettin' hurt and shit. Just go home.*

Oh, you can stay but I can't? Really?

Yeah. Vinny, look, we'll be right to the crib after this, aight. Just go home and stay there.

Why?

Because I need somebody there for Prince in case something happens to me, aight?!

It was probably better that we were texting because if we were face to face, my emotions might have gotten the best of me and I would've become physical with him. Not that I would've overpowered him or anything like that, I just didn't want to be in a position where something like that could happen between us. I loved him too much for us to even go there. He looked up at me as I peered over the steering wheel in his direction. He shook his head and moments later, he peeled out of the parking lot, screeching the tires as he left. A few people around us flinched and prepared themselves to hit the ground in case it was a drive by. Typical behavior for individuals in the hood and if they didn't do it, I would've questioned if I was really in the gutter or not.

I finally got a text from Loc,

Where you at?

Qwik Mart around the corner.

Moments later, they showed up three cars deep. Loc waved me over to him as I got out and headed in his direction. Two men in the back of his truck were loading clips into pistols and rounds into shotguns, passing them around to other men in the car when they were ready to be fired. "Where?" Loc asked as he continued looking out the front window.

"It's just around the corner; it's the second house on the right at the end of the block. There should have been a bunch of Mexicans out there on the block just chillin'."

"Let's roll."

"Wait, how we gon' do this shit?"

He glared at me like I just asked an absurdity,

"We go in there; we kill everything in our way, and we get the boy back."

"Wait, we can't just go in there blazin', we don't know where Prince is. One of the bullets could hit him."

He looked at me, waiting for me to continue,

"I think we need to start a commotion with the Mexicans if they still chillin' out there. Like one or two of us, and it's better if it doesn't lead to anybody getting shot. While their attention is distracted, then we send two more people to the front door and knock. Tell whoever answers that they are looking for Keyonna and say it's one of Big Tuck's boys, and they are comin' to pick up Prince. Now, if they look at the two guys crazy like, *who the fuck is Prince?*, then we know he ain't there, and we can roll. But if they go back and get her, then we know he is in there."

He kept his eyes focused on the front windshield. I knew he was paying attention to me, but he never gave affirmations that he was. I was used to him, so I continued,

"Then, if there is any resistance, the niggas who went inside the house pulls out and handles up. By that time, them Mexicans on the corner will probably turn to run to the house, and that's when the niggas that were on the corner with them takes them out while they aren't looking. While all that is happening, I'ma sneak through the back. It's a window that is cracked open that overlooks the backyard. I don't know if they got security back there or not because I couldn't see everything over the fence, but if it is, I know all the commotion in the front will draw them away. After that, it's on me."

Loc didn't say anything for a few moments. I heard some of the guys in the back laugh when I finished up, and I couldn't tell if they were laughing because it was a good idea or if it was one of the dumbest things they've heard, but whichever one it was, I didn't care. We needed some plan before we just went onto their block with bad intentions. An intoxicated man exited the gas station as I sat, waiting for Loc to respond. He had stumbled down the sidewalk before he fell flat on the ground, smacking his face into the pavement. Another man walked outside, laughing and pointing at him, "Get yo' drunk ass up, muthafucka! Shit! You done knocked the teeth out yo' mouth with ya' dumbass!" He helped him to his feet as two of his teeth remained on the ground while they walked away. I turned back to Loc. "Get in. Let's roll," he said, rolling up his window before I could respond.

Dusk was setting in as we pulled up on the block. Loc sent two of the trucks ahead of us as they went and parked just across the street from the house. The Mexicans were still gathered outside on the corner as two of our men got out the truck and walked in their direction. I couldn't tell what was going on, but I watched intensely as they began to make a small commotion with the SA's. Soon after, three of our men got out of the car and walked to the house unabated as the Mexicans attention was kept close to the distraction. Our guys stood at the door for a few moments when suddenly, one of the Mexicans unexpectedly turned around. He put his hands up and walked over to the porch where our guys stood. Just then, that one Mexican went inside as the men on the porch sent a signal back to us, sending us around through the alley. -We parked a few houses down from our targeted house, and four of us got out the car while one man stayed in the driver's seat, ready to peel off as soon as we got out.

The streetlights flickered on as we crept through the alley. A cat knocked over a small trash can and sprinted away as we inched past the house. I was the only one to flinch, but I quickly regained my focus and kept up with them. When we got to the fence, I held my hand up, signaling for them to stop. I ducked down and peeked through the boards on the fence. I couldn't see anything moving around back there, no dogs, no other people, nothing at all. Loc put his hand down to boost me over the fence, and he lifted me up in one swift motion and just like that, I was over. I went to the gate and unlocked the door, thinking at any moment I was going to hear gunshots, but still there was nothing. Loc and the other guy with him snuck into the gate as we crept to the window. Suddenly, out of nowhere, two Rottweilers charged at us, barking and growling like they were ready to devour us. Loc's man shot at them piercing them right in the head one after the other. The gunshots echoed throughout the hood and for a split second, it was quiet. The calm before the storm and I knew this storm was going to be ferocious. Immediately after that, gunshots could be heard from the front of the house. I ran to the window and hopped through as the bullets were being fired in every direction. My mind went to Prince because with all these stray bullets, one could pierce him at any moment. I stumbled over a table when I got in as Loc and his guys ran to the back door for me to open it. I popped the lock and froze, not knowing which way to go. There was a staircase that led upstairs and just in the middle of a hallway there was a door. It seemed like it led to a basement or something but I couldn't decide which way to go. I choose to go to the basement and, through a brief silence in the gunfire, I heard a baby's cry come from upstairs.

I spun around on a dime and headed up, skipping handfuls of steps at a time. There were only three rooms to choose from and as I pulled my pistol out, I opened the first door and to my surprise, Prince was sitting up in the bed, crying. "Prince," I said, lowering my pistol as my eyes began to water. When I was halfway to him, a blunt object crashed into the back of my head and caused me to fall forward into the dresser. I flipped over on my back as Keyonna stood over me with a lead pipe. I glanced up at Prince as he reached for me.

When I tried to get up, Keyonna struck me again, this time, knocking me in my chest.

"Yeah, bitch. You want to set muthafuckas up, huh? How it feel now, huh? How does it feel to," she picked up the pipe and swung again as I used my forearms to defend myself, "know the one you love is the one that got you set up, huh? This little nigga right here got you into some shit that you won't be able to make it out of alive. Yeah. I told Big Tuck at his grave that I would get you back for this shit!"

The gunfire kept going off below me and I knew it was just a matter of time before I was killed or the police showed up. Either way, it was going to be over. She swung the pipe again as it came crashing down onto my collarbone. Prince cried on the bed as the gunfire eventually came to silence. She lifted the pipe again, but I rolled out of the way as it smacked into the dresser that was right behind me. I quickly scooted over to the gun that flew under the bed and cocked it, aiming it straight at her. I barely had enough strength to load the bullet into the chamber, but I did, and she stood over me, just a few feet away breathing heavily with the pipe in her hand.

"You a smart muthafucka," she said, smiling. "All I wanna know is how you found out that that little nigga was here. Shit, the fun hadn't even gotten started yet."

"Fuck you, bitch. I should've let Nas do yo' ass when he had the chance."

"Nas," she laughed, "Right. The nigga that… is most likely going to kill you anyway for getting his son kidnapped. Yeah, that Nas, right? No, bitch, YOU should've killed him when you had the chance because now, that nigga will kill you. Trust me. The bug has been put in his ear."

Prince's cries became louder as I slowly raised myself up from the floor and peered at her from the barrel of my gun.

Before I knew it, my finger contracted around the trigger, and I fired three shots in her direction. They all went right into her head, and her body collapsed onto the floor. I stood over her and emptied the rest of the clip into her purely from rage. I looked over at Prince as he sat on the bed, his eyes full of tears and ready to burst again as I put the gun back on my waist and grabbed him with the one arm that I could use. The heat from the pistol burned my waist as I winced, carrying Prince down the stairs. When I got to the bottom, there were dead bodies everywhere. Some of our guys but mostly it was theirs. I walked out the back as police sirens increased their volume but to my surprise, the truck I rode in with Loc was gone from the alley. *Oh my, God*, I said to myself, *this nigga left me?* I looked to my right as a car flicked on its headlights. I reached for my pistol as it rolled down the alley but I was relieved when I saw who was driving.

"I thought I told yo' ass to go home."

"Shut the fuck up and get in the car."

He helped me get in the back seat as I laid sideways. As Vinny drove away, the streetlights above me passed over my head in five-second intervals, illuminating Prince. His face made me forget any pain I had and everything else that was going on in my life. He sat on the seat next to where I lay, not crying, not fussing or anything. He was expressionless and even though he wasn't even a year old yet, he had probably been through more in his life than a lot of grown men. The thing that scared me the most was how calm he was. As the lights passed over us and shined into the car, he didn't look much like Junie anymore. At some point that had all gone away. Now, when I looked at him, he looked exactly like Nas, and it scared the shit out of me. *I have my boy back*, I said to myself, *he is safe*. The only question I had now was what happens next.

Chapter 13

For the next few days, I laid low so I could recover. I didn't go to the hospital for them to check on my injuries. I had nothing but bad memories every time I'd visited there so if I could stand to stay away, then I would. I didn't hear from Loc or anybody since I had gotten Prince. I didn't know if Nas decided to bury the hatchet or not but if I had to guess, I would say that he didn't. The man he had turned into was not the man I met back at Remy's concert over a year ago. He completely changed, and I didn't know if it was because of the drug lord mentality getting the best of him or if it was simply because I crossed him with Prince. Either way, I knew the romantic chapter of my life with him was over. I stayed away from Big Mama's house because I knew that if they were going to try to do something to me that would be the first place they would look. I checked myself into a hotel and remained there for a few days. I told Mrs. Butler and Vinny where I was just in case they needed to find me, but I didn't want to put them in any more danger than they needed to be. Mrs. Butler visited us a few times. Allen's funeral was a few days ago and it hurt me to not be able to attend, but for obvious reasons I couldn't. She walked into my hotel room and immediately went to Prince, "Hey, honey. Hey Grandma's baby!" she said to him as she lifted him into the air. Ever since I'd brought him back with me, he hadn't smiled as much as he used to. It was almost like he was an entirely different baby than he was before. He wasn't the jovial bundle of joy that we had grown to love and maybe the events he went through in these past couple weeks were traumatic enough to affect him, even at his young age.

"I don't know what's wrong with him, Mom."

"Oh, he'll be alright. He's just been through a lot. He'll snap out of it."

When she found out about Prince being kidnapped, it was after I had gotten him back. I didn't think she would be able to handle all of the emotional stress at once, so I did my best to protect her from it. She was angry but more importantly, she was just grateful that he was back in the right hands. I tried to sit up in my bed, but the pain shot through my shoulder as I winced

"Baby, maybe you need to go and get yourself checked out. Your collarbone could be broken."

"Nah, I'm good Mama. I'll be fine. I just need some time, that's all."

"Do you want me to take Prince for a few days?"

"No," I said abruptly, "I mean, no, it's ok. I'll keep him here with me. He'll be fine."

"Ok, baby. I understand, trust me."

"How is Serena doing?"

"She's…. she's doing the best she can right now, I guess. You know, she's trying to keep herself busy with work and everything."

"She was a mess when I saw her at the house last week."

"Yeah, she… she took it hard. I mean, she did start carrying that little pistol around, though. I honestly can't tell if it is for protection or if she does it because her father bought it for her. I don't know which is which but all I can say is that I'm glad she has it."

"Yeah, me too."

Mrs. Butler left later that night, and I was happy that she visited me. It felt like I was in somewhat of a hospital already because I never left the room. Anything I needed, Vinny or Mrs. Butler brought it to me so I could stay in and rest. That's what they would tell me, but deep inside, I knew they were doing it because they didn't want me to end up shot dead. "Hey Mama's baby," I said to Prince as he sat up in my bed. He turned towards me with a lock-lipped expression on his face. Nothing I said or did could make him smile and eventually, he turned his head back towards the television. "What is wrong with you?" I asked him just under my breath. I reached out to rub his leg as I gingerly laid down on top of the bed and moments later, I had fallen asleep.

I woke up to Prince's laughter as he sat in Nas's arms in the hotel room. I jumped up and threw my back into the headboard as my eyes bucked open in horror. Nas turned to look at me, "He aight, Lyric. He just wanted to see his daddy, that's all." They both looked towards me with the same eerie smile escaping their lips. "How have you been?" Nas asked as he got up and sat on the bed next to me. I scooted away and remained quiet.

"Oh, so you're not speaking to me? What a shame. What happened to us, Lyric? We used to be so tight. Remember when we first had sex down at the lakefront. Now that I think about it, it's probably the time we conceived little old Prince. Yup, it sure was. We were just about inseparable then, you know what I'm saying? What happened?"

He reached for me, but I jerked my leg out of his grasp. "Ok, I get it. You're afraid of me, right? You think I'm going to hurt you?" He laughed as he kissed Prince on the cheek, "Listen, I'm not going to put my hands on you anymore. Well, I'm going to try not to anyway. You see, my son loves you, and I never want him to see me hurt you or anything like that. I don't want him to SEE it. Are you paying attention, Lyric? I mean, as long as he doesn't see it, it should be fine, right?"

"Nas, what did I do to you for you to treat me like this, huh? What did I do?"

He smiled and looked at Prince, "Oh, she speaks now," he said as Prince giggled, "your mother speaks. What did you do? Well, first of all, you protected an enemy who clearly was ready to drop the dime on us. If not you, then definitely me. On top of that, you stayed in this city when I told you to leave and what happened? You ended up getting my only son kidnapped and almost killed. You crossed me, Lyric. Not to mention the shit you tried to pull in front of Man-Man at the stash house. Disrespecting me like that? No, not in front of my people. It just seems as though you've worn out your welcome, you know what I'm saying?"

"Look, whatever you're going to do, just do it, aight? I'm tired of this shit. I've had enough of living like this. You want me, then here I am."

He laughed, "The thing is, Lyric, I already got you. You are as good as dead; you just don't know it… but you will. Slowly but surely, you will know."

I jumped up off my bed and immediately, the pain shot through my shoulder blade, almost paralyzing me. Prince looked over at me as he sat in the same position he was in when I dozed off. I wasn't sure how long I had been asleep, but it couldn't have been for long because the same TV show that was on before I went to sleep was still on now. Prince turned back around and laid backward on the bed. I reached for the bottle that was on the nightstand and handed it to him, but he turned over on his side, completely rejecting it. "Alright Mama's baby, alright. I understand," I said as I placed it back on the shelf. I hated that he totally flipped into another child since being kidnapped, but I couldn't blame him. In reality, I could only blame myself. If I had just left like Nas told me to do in the beginning, none of this would have happened. Maybe Mr. Butler would still be alive and Nas and I probably wouldn't even be at odds, but I couldn't live on hypotheticals; I had to live with facts, and the fact was that Nas doesn't forget and forgive, so I knew I had to get out of the city.

Prince and I slept all night in the same spots on the bed until housekeeping woke us the next morning. "No, I'm good, come back later," I yelled out to her after she knocked on the door. Prince opened his eyes with a look of panic when he heard my voice. He reached up above him as if he was trying to pull himself up and that's when I sat up in the bed, the pain radiated through my collarbone, but I didn't give any thought to it. He gasped for air as I pulled him up to a seated position. His eyes scanned the room and then suddenly, tears fell from his eyes and he screamed out with gut-wrenching cries. I grabbed him and put my good arm around him, but he squirmed and fought me off as if he didn't recognize me. "Prince, Prince, it's mommy! It's ok, it's Mommy!" I said frantically as he continued to swing his arms and legs to try to get away from me. I held him as tight as I could and rocked him as he continued screaming. Eventually, tears began to fall from my eyes and onto the top of his head. "What did they do to my baby", I said out loud, "what did they do to him?!" He cried out loud, and I wasn't able to console him, and it was one of the most helpless feelings I'd ever had in my life.

Chapter 14

Later that day, I called Vinny to come to the hotel room after he got off work. When he walked in, Prince was still crying, and he had been doing it off and on ever since he woke up this morning. Sometimes, he would just whine as though he was irritated, but other times it was a flat-out scream at the top of his lungs as if he was in pain. Vinny walked into the room, "Damn, what's wrong with Prince?" he asked as he walked over to him on the bed. Prince's face was completely covered in tears, and his nose was running. "I don't know. I mean, he doesn't have a fever or anything, and when I checked his symptoms on the internet, none of it was making sense to me." Vinny picked him up into his arms as Prince's screams simmered down a little bit.

"Maybe he's teething?" he said, "Did you check his gums?"

"Yeah, I felt around in there, and I didn't feel any teeth. I don't know Vinny; I think they did something to my baby when they had him. He's been acting funny ever since I got him back."

"Well, he's been through a lot. Even for a baby, you know? I mean, we would think that since he's not even one yet that none of that stuff would affect him, but children are hard to read sometimes."

Vinny rocked Prince, and it seemed as if it only took him a few moments to completely stop crying and begin to fall asleep. I looked over at him, "That's fucked up. I've been rocking him like that all damn morning, and that little nigga wasn't trying to have none of it from me."

Vinny laughed, "You just don't have that touch, I guess. I mean, the ladies tell me I have that touch so a nigga must have that touch, you know what I'm saying?"

"Whatever nigga. But yo, I think I'm going to leave the city, though. I'm starting to think I have to."

"Why? Whassup?"

"Well, first of all, I can't stay in the fuckin' hotel forever. I'ma have to leave eventually, and second, look outside real quick."

Vinny got up and walked over to the window of my fifth-floor room, still cradling Prince. "Aight, what am I looking at?" he asked. I gingerly walked over to the window; my collarbone was still sore from Keyonna hitting me. "You see that truck? All white with the tinted windows way down there?" He squinted his eyes as he looked to the left, "Yeah."

"Well, I been watching the lot pretty much since I been here but for the past two days, that fuckin' truck has been showing up and parking in the same spot. I know somebody is in there because I saw the door open and close when I was peeping it from the window. I don't think they could tell I was looking because they didn't change anything about what they were doing, but I believe that they've been watching me."

"How you know something like that is going on?"

"Vinny, sometimes you just gotta follow your intuition, you know what I'm saying? I mean, shit, you know about that. You followed the same intuition when I told yo' ass to go back home, but you stayed and parked in the alley to wait for me. Shit, if you weren't there, then I woulda' got hemmed up by the police."

I grabbed his shirt and led him away from the window, "So, I'm just saying, I got a feeling that Nas sent some of his boys after me to get rid of me and get his son back, and all they are doing is plotting how to do it. But one thing I can do myself is plot, you feel me? So, I'm trying to stay a few steps ahead of them." He laid Prince down on the bed. He started to whine again, but it stopped quickly as he closed his eyes and went back to sleep. "Aight, so what you wanna do?" Vinny asked. I glanced at Prince before answering,

"I'm gonna leave out of this hotel, but I need somebody to take Prince out with them first. I don't want him with me if they happen to track me down. He needs to be safe somewhere else."

"That's cool. So, when? Now?"

"Tomorrow. I gotta set some stuff up first in another city."

"Where are you going?"

"I think I'ma head back to Chicago."

"You sure? I mean, you know what—"

"Yeah, I know what happened to me there, but Chicago is a big enough city to hide in, so I'll be alright."

"You want me to come with you for a minute like I was going to before?"

I looked over at Prince as he laid asleep on the bed, "You know what, that's cool. I mean, it seems like you're the only one that could put him to sleep like that so, yeah. I'ma check with Mrs. Butler first though and see what she thinks about it and then I'll hit you back later tonight, aight?"

"That's cool."

"Aight."

Vinny plopped down in the chair next to the bed and flipped through the television with the remote control. I walked back over to the window and peeked behind the curtains, still watching for the white truck that was there before. Suddenly, the truck pulled out of its spot and rolled slowly through the parking lot. I moved away from the window as it crept past my room and into the main street. I knew they would be back, and I had to be sure I was gone when they did.

Vinny left at almost midnight, and Prince had just woken up when he did. I was dreading another episode of Prince screaming at the top of his lungs but to my surprise, he was quiet. I reached out to him as he sat up on the bed, looking around as if he was trying to remember where he was. He saw my outstretched arms but didn't reach back. I felt a small part of me crumble as he turned away and looked at the television. Shaking my head, I got up and walked to my phone that was plugged up to the charger just a few feet away from the bed. I began searching for areas of Chicago I could move to temporarily, but there was nothing that came up that fit what I was looking for. Everything was too expensive or in the heart of the city, and I knew that neither would be an option for me right now. I walked back over to the window to see if the white suburban was parked outside again but the lot was still clear of it. I called Mrs. Butler. She told me that no matter what her line was always open to me, and it didn't matter the time of night. I was grateful for that as I reached out to her. "Hello?" She sounded as if she was sleeping.

"I'm sorry, Mom, did I wake you?"

"Lyric? No, it's alright baby, it's alright. What is it? Are you in trouble? Is Prince ok?"

I could tell she was becoming frantic, "Mom, everything is Ok. Prince is fine. I was just reaching out to you because I decided to move out of the city. I was going to go to Chicago, but I realize that it may not be the best choice."

I waited for her to gather herself, "Ok. Yes, Chicago might not be the best place for you. My guess is that you want to leave the state but stay close?"

"Yes, Ma'am."

"How about Peoria? It's a bit further out than Chicago, but it is a tiny, peaceful city. I would imagine that you could go there and start completely over without anything to impede your steps."

"Peoria? I've never heard of that city."

"Oh, it's nice. I've been there once or twice with Allen. It's very quaint, and I don't know how well you will adjust to it being a city girl, you, but there is not another place in Illinois that I would recommend over Peoria. If you'd like, I can drive you there."

"Let me look into it first so I can see what I can afford there."

"Ok, honey. You just let me know, and I'll make plans, alright?"

"Yes, Ma'am."

"Was there anything else?"

I glanced over at Prince as his eyes began to bubble with tears. "No, Mom, I'm good. I'm going to get some rest now, ok? I'll call you tomorrow." I rushed her off the phone before Prince burst into cries again. I picked him up and rocked him the way Vinny did, but it wasn't what he wanted. His cries became louder as I sighed and tears fell out my eyes. It was going to be a long night for the both of us.

It took a few hours for Prince to calm down and it was around 4 am when I researched Peoria, Illinois. There was only about 116,000 people there and the crime rate was extremely low. The housing was affordable for me and even if I didn't work for the next year, the money I had saved up would be enough to pay rent and my other bills for that time. *This is the place*, I said to myself. I walked back over to the window to check the parking lot once more. The suburban wasn't out there. Maybe I was tripping. Maybe that car wasn't full of Nas's men, and I was just paranoid. Either way, I knew I still had to leave because I had no idea what Nas was going to be up to once he was released. I knew he wanted Prince, but I wasn't in a position to hand him over. The only way he would be able to get him is if I was dead, and I think he fully understood that and was preparing for it to happen. I walked back over to the bed and gently laid down, being careful not to wake Prince up from his sleep.

As I gazed at him, the traits he had of Junie were all gone. The only person I saw when I looked at him was Nas, and it was like this whole time, I had only been imagining Junie's features in him, and now, the reality of who his father was began to set in. I took a deep breath and flipped the television off and focused on Prince, watching his belly slowly move up and down from his breathing. I prayed to God that the nasty side of Nas wasn't evolving inside of him, but only time would tell. Moments later, I was asleep.

Chapter 15

When I woke up, I wiped my eyes and walked straight over to the window to check the parking lot. The suburban still wasn't there, and now, I was entirely convinced that I was just paranoid but either way, I knew I still had to make my way out of Milwaukee. Prince was still sound asleep, so I hopped into the shower and washed myself up. My collarbone was still bruised and tender to the touch. The more I saw the discoloration of it, the more I felt that maybe I needed to get it checked out, but I still refused to go into a hospital. I knew I was just stubborn, but there were still too many bad memories for me to walk into one of those buildings on my own free will. When I turned the shower off, I heard some movement at the door, so I froze, thinking I was hearing things. As I sat and waited a few more moments, the sound was gone, so I continued what I was doing. After I wrapped the towel around myself and walked into the room, I screamed and fell backward into the door. Loc sat on the bed with Prince in his arms, still asleep. I looked around the room, expecting to see other men in there but he was the only one. "Loc, Loc, what the fuck? How the fuck did you get in here?!" He didn't say a word as he cradled Prince in his arms, rocking him slowly. The way he held him was beyond me. I never knew a man like him would be able to hold a baby as delicately as he was right now. "Loc? Loc!" I yelled to get his attention, but he kept staring down at Prince, making sure he was ok.

I walked over to my nightstand and quickly pulled the gun out from the drawer and aimed it right at him, "Loc, put Prince down. I'm not fuckin' playin', and you know I'm not. I will fuckin' kill you without thinking twice before you walk out of here with my son." Loc lifted his head in my direction; not one facial expression was detected from him. A cold, stone-faced glare that showed no signs of fear or worries of death. "If I wanted Prince or wanted you dead, it would already be done."

I walked closer to him, aiming the pistol directly at him, saying, "Fuck all that shit, Loc. Put Prince down, man. Please." He slowly laid Prince down on the bed and stood up, looming over me like a giant. His skin was dark like an oily river, his lips were dark and pursed together. His eyes were dark and unforgiving like he had taken the souls of many people before now. He took a step towards me, but I cocked the pistol, causing him to freeze in his steps. Prince moved around on the bed and then suddenly stopped and went back to sleep. Loc never took his eyes off me as I glanced away to make sure Prince was okay. *He could have killed me if he wanted to*, I thought to myself; *he's not here to hurt me*. It didn't seem like he was but I couldn't be too sure.

"The white suburban outside. Why do you think it hasn't come back?"

I didn't respond to him as I waited for him to explain himself, the pistol still aimed at him. The whole time he watched me, he was fearless. It was like the thought of death didn't impede his actions in any way, and the same, cold-faced glare looked right back into my eyes. "I killed them. They were sent here to finish the job I didn't." I wrinkled my eyebrow, "The job you didn't?"

"I was supposed to kill you the day you went to get Prince. After you had got him, I was expected to murder you and take him with me. Everybody knew it, but I couldn't go through with it. The way you risked your life for your son. How you put yourself in danger and was ready to face whatever consequence just as long as he was safe? It reminded me of a woman that was very special to me. I figured I would just let the police arrest you and put you away so Prince would be out of your hands."

I relaxed the gun in my hand, "Who? What woman?"

"It's not important. What you need to do is get the fuck out of the city."

"I know that already, Loc. I was planning on it."

"Plan quicker. I'm here to tell you that Nas is not fuckin' around. He wants his son back. He wants him raised around him and his people so he will be sure that Prince will follow in his footsteps. You already know he is willing to kill you to make it happen."

"Shit, Loc. Shit! What the fuck did I do to that nigga?"

"He is big on loyalty, and once that shit is gone, you're dead to him."

"How the fuck are you still alive then?"

"It takes more than a few men to kill me."

"Are you leaving the city, too?"

"No. I'd rather live on my feet than die on my knees, and before you try to use the same shit to stay here, you got a son to think about now. If I had a kid, maybe it would be different for me, but I don't. You got Prince to think about, and you need to get the fuck out the city."

"I know. Prince is the only reason I'm leaving this muthafucka. If it weren't for him, then I would just be here waiting for Nas ass."

He walked past me like a boulder, "I'll drive you out of town just to be safe." I placed the gun on the nightstand, "I need to make a couple stops first, Loc. I have to say my goodbyes." His gaze was relentless,

"We don't have time for that shit, Lyric."

"Fuck that! I'm stopping with or without you, Loc. I'll do this shit myself if I have to."

He glared at me as his jawbones gyrated inside his mouth, "I'll be outside in a Black Escalade," and with that, the door shut and he was gone. I looked at Prince as he was just beginning to wake up. I didn't want to leave by any means, but the way Loc was talking, Nas was coming for me with a full head of steam, so I didn't have a choice. I got dressed and got Prince ready to go as quickly as I could with only one good arm. I slid my pistol in my waistband and moments later, we were out the door. Loc sat in his truck, just beyond the front door of the hotel. I looked around before I walked to it. He got out and let me in the back and with that, we took off. "Big Mama's crib, Loc." I could tell he wasn't happy about it, but he went anyway.

Vinny's car was parked in the driveway when I got there. I walked to the door, cradling Prince in my good arm. He hadn't cried once since he woke up this morning and that was a big turnaround from the past few days. Vinny came to the door, "Whassup Lyric?" He let me in as I walked into the front room. Prince reached for Vinny as soon as he saw him. "I think you got a new best friend," I said as he took Prince in his arms. "No doubt, no doubt," Vinny said with a smile. He looked out the door at the car that was parked on the street,

"Who in the car, Lyric?"

"It's Loc."

"Loc?? The fuck you mean, Loc? Loc, as is Nas's boy, Loc?"

"Yo, chill Vinny, chill. He's good."

"Nah, Lyric. Fuck that shit. You say he's good, and then you end up dead somewhere, and Prince is gone."

"Look, I got this shit, aight? Trust me. I'm smarter than that. I felt this nigga out already; he's good."

Vinny held Prince as he peered at me, completely uncomfortable with what I was doing but he had no choice but to accept it. Since I was going to Peoria, he knew he wouldn't be able to make the trip because it was too far away. He didn't have as much vacation time as he thought so it all would have been a wash. Two days wasn't long enough for him to stay in the city with me. I walked to Big Mama's room. It was just as peaceful as I remembered. I hadn't been to the house in a while, but I could still feel the nostalgia that came every time I stepped foot into the room. Everything was still the same as I walked around, running my hand over the surface of the dresser. I sighed when I got to my mother's picture as it leaned against the mirror outside of its frame. I thought about Uncle Stew and how he died the same way she did. The guilt was still on my conscious, and I was saddened even more by the fact that we left him there, but it was too much going on to do anything else about it. It was just too much going on and all I could do was hope he understood.

"Hey, Big Mama. I was going to go to your grave, but then I figured that coming here would be better. It just feels like this is where you always are anyway, you know? So, here I am," I smiled, more to hide the pain than anything else, "so, I'm finally leaving. It took a lot, but I finally got the point. I don't know why I was so hard headed but hey, I wouldn't be Lyric if I wasn't, right? I'm going to Peoria. You ever heard of it? You probably have, but that's where I'm going. It's quiet there, so hopefully, I can stay out of trouble. I'm taking Prince with me, too. I thought about leaving him here with Mrs. Butler, but I figured that Nas would find him there a lot quicker than he would if he was with me. For some reason, he has been acting funny, though. Ever since I got him back, he's been crying and whining almost non-stop. I don't know what it is, but I know that if you were here, you would figure it out. You were always good at that kind of stuff. You just had that loving touch, I guess. But from the looks of it, Vinny has the same thing."

Just then, I heard movement at Big Mama's door. I turned around to see Vinny holding Prince, still hesitant to come in. I shook my head and waved him over, "Dude, just come in. You're like a son to Big Mama; I don't know why you're always acting like that." He walked in with Prince, looking around like he was walking onto sacred ground, "You know how I am, though. I just don't want to mess nothing up, you see?" I took Prince out of his arms as he smiled bright enough to light up the room we were in. "See Big Mama," I said, "he's already smiling like you were here." I wiped a tear from my eye as we all stood in the room, quietly, just taking in the ambiance that was flowing around us. This was the one thing that I would miss the most out of everything in Milwaukee. This house, this room, and this feeling. It would never be replaced, not by anything or anyone else. We said our goodbyes to Vinny, and I let him know that I would be back to visit as soon as things settled down. He fought back tears as he walked us to the door. He was my ace, and I knew that I could trust him to take care of Big Mama's house. He would have never moved in if I thought that he couldn't.

The last stop was Mrs. Butler's home. Loc was visibly becoming bothered by the brief farewell tour, but I let him know that he could leave whenever he wanted to. In the back of my mind, I hoped he wouldn't call my bluff because I knew that, if my back was against the wall, I could count on him to help me out. We walked to Mrs. Butler's door. She knew I was coming because I gave her a heads-up of my plans earlier that day. She made sure that Serena would be home that day so she could get her goodbyes in as well. Mrs. Butler opened the door, and Prince immediately smiled as big and bright as he could. "Grandma's baby!" she said as she twirled him around in the air. Serena came out of the back, her pistol in the holster that was wrapped around her hip. I smiled,

"Ok, Serena. I see the pistol is like your best friend now." She laughed, "Yeah, I mean, I guess I just got used to it being on me."

"Have you had to use it yet?"

"Not really. I mean, I took it to the gun range with Mama a few days ago but other than that I haven't had to shoot anybody. But I think taking me to the range was the wrong thing to do because now, I do have an urge to shoot somebody."

"Oh Lord," Mrs. Butler said as she sat down on the couch with Prince, "this girl is losing it."

Serena walked over to Prince and pinched his dimple, "Oh my goodness, he is so cute! I'm going to miss seeing his cute little face around here!" I glanced towards her, "So, all that means is you have to have one of your own now." She paused, "Uh, sorry. Wrong chick," she said, "I'm not ready for all that yet. I need a couple more years to enjoy my freedom!" Her mom interjected, "Girl, in a few years, you'll be 30 and trust me; you are not going to want to push out any children by the time you're 30." It didn't take me long to lose track of the time.

"Shoot! We need to get going!"

Mrs. Butler's sadness clearly showed, "Oh, alright. I'm not prepared to say goodbye," she said as she squeezed Prince one last time.

"It's not goodbye, mom. It's more like, see you later."

"You're right. If push comes to shove, I'll be making a few trips out there to see you guys."

"Trust me, you'll be welcomed. Prince is just in love with you."

"Ohhh! And I am so in love with his little itty-bitty self! You're grandma's baby, aren't you? Yes, you are! Yes, you are!"

She kissed him as he laughed and giggled, gobs of saliva traveling down his mouth. She peeked in as he held it open, "Uhh, Lyric? This baby has teeth coming in!" I looked towards him, "What? Teeth? Where?" She held his mouth open and showed me where some of them were peeking in toward the back. She asked,

"He hasn't been crying and acting funny?"

"Oh my goodness, Mom! That's all he has been doing! I mean, I checked his symptoms but he wasn't running a fever, and I didn't see any teeth, so I didn't think he was teething."

"Oh no, honey. This baby is teething, and they are about ready to come in. I'm going to give you some of this children's Tylenol I have back here to take with you. That should help take away some of that pain. Here, sit tight and we will be right back."

I was relieved at the fact that teething was the cause of all his screaming. The whole time, I thought it was something that I was doing wrong to him or that maybe they did something to him when he was kidnapped. As she went to the back, I walked to the front door to check on Loc. To my surprise, he was gone. I wrinkled my brow as I opened the door and stepped outside to get a better look. *Maybe he pulled down the block a little bit;* I said to myself as I moved to the sidewalk. I didn't see his truck anywhere as a mist saturated the atmosphere. "Fuck!" I said out loud, rechecking the block for him, hoping that his truck would turn from around the corner and head back this way. I called his cell phone, but it was disconnected, and I had no other way to get in touch with him. After I waited a few moments and he still didn't show up, I turned to walk back inside the house. Mrs. Butler was giving Prince some of the medicine she had gotten from the back, "Now Lyric," she said,

"Only give him about 1.5 ML of this. It's marked here on the little syringe. You don't want to overdose him."

"Mom, my ride left."

She paused, "Left? What do you mean left?"

"He just took off. I went to look outside to make sure he was ok, and he was gone."

"Who was it, Vinny? I'ma call that boy right now and—"

"No, it wasn't Vinny."

"Then who was it? Tell them to come back."

I was reluctant to say who it was because I knew she would flip out. Eventually, Mrs. Butler agreed to drive me out to Peoria herself. Now that Loc had suddenly left the way he did, I started to question his sincerity. What if he just wanted to find out where I was going? What if it was all a setup? I found myself in a daze, thinking about the possibly as Mrs. Butler placed Prince in my lap and said, "We're going to leave early tomorrow morning, ok? So just sit tight for the rest of the day and then we will head out. I need to rest up for the drive." I didn't want to wait that long, but it was the only option. She wasn't ready to make such a long trip on such short, and I couldn't do anything but respect it. At the same time, I was worried about the danger I could be bringing to their home. If Loc was still working with Nas, he would know exactly where I was at and could easily finish the job.

As Mrs. Butler walked out of the front room, I placed Prince down in his playpen and headed back to the window, hoping to see his truck back outside, but there was nothing. The rain fell hard onto the pavement, abusing everything that was exposed to it. The pain radiated through my collarbone once again, causing me to wince. I turned around as Prince stood up in his playpen, bouncing up and down and seemingly back to his normal behavior. I sat down on the couch next to him as he bounced up and down, looking more and more like Nas by the day. I kissed him on the cheek and laid down on the couch as he laughed and yelled in the background. There was no way I was going to get a wink of sleep that night. My hand was going to stay close to the pistol and ready to fire at the drop of a dime.

Chapter 16

"Baby, how long have you been up?"

"Hey, Mom. I've been up for a while. I just couldn't sleep."

It was five when she saw me sitting on the couch, flipping through channels with the remote control. Prince was on the sofa next to me, sound asleep with my hand on his back. The truth is that I was dead tired, but I just couldn't sleep comfortably because I didn't know what Loc had going on. I still didn't understand why he risked so much just to leave me at Mrs. Butlers house. It wasn't making sense to me, but I didn't want to stick around and find out why. Throughout the night, I searched for another city to move to since I already told Loc I was going to Peoria. If he were trying to set me up, he would have to find me somewhere else. I wasn't going to be a sitting duck for anyone.

"Ok. Well, just give me a minute to get a bite to eat and we will head out."

"That's fine. Oh, and Ma, there's been a change of plans. I'm going to go to Rockford."

"Rockford? Why the change?"

"Oh, I just think that that city will be better for me. I mean, Peoria is far, and Rockford just seems like it will be better for me and Prince."

She stood at the bottom of the staircase with a perplexed look scattered across her face. I could tell she was trying to make sense of it all, and I know she was looking for a better explanation for everything, but I had nothing to give her. She wasn't going to know the truth; I was just going to tell her the bare minimum so I could get moving as quickly as possible.

"Ok, baby. Well, Rockford, it is. If that was the case, we could have left last night. Rockford is not that far at all."

"I'm sorry."

"No, no. No apologies needed, you have to make sure you and Prince will be somewhere that you're comfortable being, and if it is Rockford, then it is Rockford."

She smiled and walked into the kitchen as I laid my head back on the couch, wanting to get some sleep but still not at ease enough to let my eyes close. I glanced outside; the street lights still lit the paths up and down the neighborhood, but there was still no sign of Loc or anybody else. At this point, I just wanted to leave as quickly as possible. It didn't take long for Mrs. Butler to grab something to eat and get ready to go. When she came downstairs, I had Prince fed and ready to go out the door. "My, you sure did get him ready fast." "Quicker than I normally do! Well, alright, if you're ready, then I'm ready," she said as she reached down to pick up the diaper bag. I walked out first, surveying the area for anything unusual. After that, we got in the car and headed out of town.

As soon as we got out of Milwaukee, I finally laid my head back to rest. I was on the verge of being up for 24 hours straight, so I knew it wasn't going to take much for me to fall asleep. I heard Mrs. Butler speaking to me before I unintentionally faded away into a dreamland. When I opened my eyes again, we were at a gas station. Nothing around me looked familiar as I sat in the car observing my surroundings. Suddenly, I spun around to look in the back seat. Prince's car seat was still there, so I reached back to check if he was in there. He giggled as soon as I touched him, bringing me a sigh of relief. Moments later, the driver's side door opened, "Lyric? Girl, I thought you were going to sleep the whole trip. Well, you just about did do it. We're only about 30 minutes away now." I pulled out my cell phone to look at the time, 11:42 am.

"I'm sorry, Mom. I was just so tired. I wanted to help you drive but—"

She got into the car and closed the door, "But nothing. You needed some rest, and I could tell you were tired because you snored a few times."

"I snored?"

She laughed, "Yes, girl. You just about scared me half to death a few times, and I almost swerved off the road."

"Oh my God, I'm so sorry."

"No, listen here. You're going to stop apologizing for every little thing that you do. I am your Mom, ok? And I expect my daughter to do certain things without needing an apology from her and snoring is one of them. Now, you go ahead and get you a little more rest. I will wake you up when we get into the city so you can tell me where you need to go. Matter of fact just put the address in my GPS."

She handed me her phone as I punched in the address of the hotel and gave it back to her. "Good, now you go ahead and get some more sleep. Prince is doing just fine keeping me company, isn't that right, Granny's baby?" He laughed and cooed at her when he heard her voice. "You see," she said, "everything is fine. I'll wake you when we get there." She started the car and pulled off as I leaned my head back once again on the headrest. I was asleep within minutes.

When Mrs. Butler woke me up, we were parked in front of the Hilton in downtown Rockford. The hotel was beautiful from the outside, and it looked like something that was right out of a movie scene. "Well, well, Lyric. You sure did pick a nice spot!" she said with a smile on her face. Suddenly, a man in navy blue slacks and a navy blue blazer approached the driver's side window. I looked at him incredulously as Mrs. Butler got out of the car and handed him the keys. I had never been anywhere with valet service before, so this was all new to me. I didn't even know they had that service here. I just looked up hotels in Rockford and picked the one that had the best rating. I took Prince out of the car, and we all headed inside the building and got the key to my room. The rooms were extravagant. The beds were large, the décor was beautiful, and I saw this place as being somewhere I wouldn't mind staying for the next week until I was able to find somewhere a bit more permanent. I sat Prince on the bed as Mrs. Butler looked around the room, stopping to admire the view from the fifth floor. "Lyric, honey, I am jealous! This is truly a beautiful place. I'm almost upset that I tried to get you to go to Peoria instead of coming here. This hotel alone is enough to get me to change my mind." I didn't care about any of that, though. My only focus was getting away from any danger that may have been coming my way in Peoria.

Ever since I left Milwaukee, I had been getting calls from unknown numbers. When I woke up in the car, I had seen that I was called back to back at least four separate times. If I were alone, I would have answered it, but I didn't know which way the call would go, and there was no need to alert Mrs. Butler. She stayed long enough to take me to the store and pick up a few clothing items and food. After that, we went to the car rental place so I could have a way to get around while I was here. When I was all squared away, we went back to the hotel room so she could get a few hours of sleep before she headed back to Milwaukee. She wrapped up in my covers with Prince as I quietly left the room, hoping the unknown number would call me back. As I sat in the lobby and waited, I called Vinny to let him know I had made it. He told me that everything was going good at Big Mama's house, but it was just too quiet for him. When Uncle Stew was there, he would at least make noise in the kitchen while he was cooking or wake the house with his terrible attempts at singing. I got the feeling that the quietness was beginning to drive him crazy, but he told me that he was alright so I just left it alone.

As I stood in the hallway, a few people walked past with smiles on their faces, seeming as if they didn't have a care in the world. I wanted to know what that feeling was like and for a moment, I envied them. Just then, my phone rang again. The unknown number called back, and I answered it right away,

"Who the fuck is this?"

"Bitch, watch yo' tone. Where the fuck are you?"

"Who the fuck is this?"

He laughed, "Oh, you don't know me now, Ma? For real?"

It took me a few seconds to recognize his voice because it had been weeks since I last spoke to him over the phone.

"Nas? You out?"

He laughed, "Bitch, wouldn't you like to know. It's funny that you think you can get away from me, though. I got eyes all over this fucking place."

"What do you want?"

"What do you mean what do I want? You got my son, don't you?"

"It's my son, too."

"Let me ask you this: Will he still be your son when you are dead?"

I sat with the phone to my ear, remaining silent as I tried to feel out the situation. I had known a lot of inmates who were able to sneak cell phones past security and with him having the type of clout he did in jail, I knew something like that wouldn't have been out of the question for him.

"Come for me then, nigga. If it's that easy, come for me."

I ended the call as I looked up and glanced at my reflection in the mirror. I was nowhere near the woman I thought I would become when I was in high school, rapping with Junie and his friends. The lady I had grown up to become was my mother. I was living the life that she would have lived out if she hadn't taken her life prematurely and I wasn't cool with it, but I had started to accept it. I knew I wasn't made to be on the side of a king; I was made to run shit on my own. I was prepared to take shit over and not have to answer to anybody. That's the side of my mother that I was living out, and as I looked at my reflection, I realized it. The phone number called back, and I sent it to voicemail. *I'll come back to Milwaukee*, I said to myself, *I just need to get a little stronger.* A little deeper and after that, I'll be back. I was by far the most strategic out of all the niggas when I was with Nas's clique, and I wasn't just going to put that shit to an end. If he wanted me, he was going to get me. Lyric, aka, Suzie Muthafuckin' Rock.

Chapter 17

A few weeks passed, and I ended up staying at the Hilton for longer than I planned. I think I just got lazy with the room service and everything, and the thought of moving out into an apartment was something that I wasn't ready to deal with. My collarbone finally healed up to the point that I could move around freely without feeling any pain. Prince was back to his normal, fun-loving self ,and as long as I had the children's Tylenol ready for him whenever his teething fits started, everything was perfect. He was even regaining some of his Junie-like facial expressions that he melted my heart with. The unknown number called my phone periodically, but I already knew who was on the other line, and I wasn't ready to answer. I wasn't willing to face him just yet, so I left it alone. *Not now, Lyric, not now*, I said to myself as it rang back to back certain times.

Even though the hotel was excellent and it was more than I could have asked for, I knew I couldn't stay there for long. Otherwise, the money that was supposed to last me for the next year would be burned up in half that time. I finally got Prince up and headed out to the north side of Rockwall to look for an apartment. It was only about a 15-minute drive from downtown Rockwall and on the way, it seemed as if I passed nothing but middle-aged and older white folks. It was something I wasn't used to, especially growing up on the north side of Milwaukee. We arrived at the apartment complex, a small, gated community with a swimming pool in the middle of it. I imagined Prince being old enough to jump into the pool with his little arm floats, swimming around with his other little friends and enjoying himself in the summer heat. Just then, Prince cooed and broke me out of my daydream. "I know, little man, I know," I said as I began walking to the apartment's office.

Inside, a short and pudgy white woman stood up with a smile that pushed her chubby cheeks up near her eyes. She walked over to me pleasantly as I held Prince in my arms, "Well, hello there! How are you?" she said, looking towards my son. He smiled back at her as she addressed me, "And hello. Welcome to Sasha's Court, how can I help you today?"

"Yes, I think I spoke with you earlier today? Are you Amy?"

"Yes, I am. And you must be Lyric Sutton?"

"Yes."

"Well, wonderful! It's great to finally put a face with the name. Come on over to my desk and we will get going with finding you a place."

We walked over to her desk and sat down as Prince reached for everything within his grasp. I had to pull him back a few times to keep him from pulling some of her things to the floor. "Oh, he is just a busy body, isn't he? Yes, he is!" she said, entertained by how active he was. "Yes, he is a handful, but he is not a problem at all." She smiled as she paged through a folder, "I'm sure he isn't! He doesn't look like one bit of trouble with those cute little dimples!" she slid the envelope in front of me,

"Ok, well, these are our floor plans for our apartments here. How many bedrooms will you be needing?"

"Either a one- or a two-bedroom will be all right."

"Ok, perfect. Well, we have both of those available now, so you're in luck! They go pretty fast, though."

I went through the floor plans and decided on which apartment I thought would fit us best and afterward she took us on a small tour of the complex and inside the apartment. It was a beautiful and cozy apartment, nothing too out of the ordinary of what I expected. We headed back to the office as she handed me the application for the apartment. I knew I didn't have income, so that was the only part that worried me about the process.

"Excuse me, Amy?"

"Yes?"

"As far as income goes, I don't have a steady income right now, but I will be able to pay eight months of rent right up front if I'm able to get this apartment leased to me."

"No steady income?"

"No, ma'am, but like I said, I can sign an eight-month lease and pay it all upfront right now."

I could tell by the look in her eyes that she was a little unsure about what I was bringing to her. She looked down at Prince as he began reaching for items on her desk again and with that, she seemed to soften up a bit, "You know what, let me take this information to the apartment supervisor and see what she says, alright? Just hold on for me once second." She got up and walked to the back of the office. I hoped that they would be able to take what I was offering because this spot couldn't have been better. It was quiet, the neighbors all smiled and waved when I was touring the facility like it was something in their lease stating that they had to. This apartment was my first choice to live, but I knew that if they didn't take the offer, somebody else around here was bound to. Over $6,000 upfront? Who in their right minds would reject that? Amy came back to her desk as I prepared myself for the worst.

"Well, I talked to the apartment supervisor, and she said that we can accept the arrangement to pay everything up front in place of you not having a steady income."

"Perfect! Thank you so much."

"No problem at all, Ms. Sutton. No problem at all."

We agreed that I would move in later that week and with that, I headed to check out the neighborhood. There were a few grocery stores just a few blocks away from the complex, so I stopped at one of them to pick up a few things to eat that night. As I strolled through the store, I caught a glimpse of a familiar face. She stood in the frozen foods aisle, seemingly stuck in-between choices. I had mixed feelings about seeing her. On one hand, I was still pissed at what she did to me in Chicago but on the other hand, it was a feeling of nostalgia that made me feel good to at least know one person in a new city. I walked up to her with my shopping cart and stood just to her side. I saw her reflection in the glass, and she laughed, her attention still straight forward, "Hell naw, Lyric. What the fuck are you doing here?" She turned around with a smile on her face as she slipped a bag of chicken into her basket, saying,

"Suzie mutha fuckin Rock. I wasn't expecting to see yo' ass anymore. You still rapping and shit?"

"Nah," I said as I stepped closer to her.

"Look, Lyric, I thought that shit between us was squashed. You remember George Webb? Shit, wasn't that enough?"

"Yeah, I just don't know what you on right now, though."

"Lyric," she smiled, reaching into the freezer for another bag of chicken, "I know I fucked you over. I get that, and that's why I didn't even come back at yo' ass after you caught me in George Webb. Yeah, I deserved that shit, but I was just jealous, you know? Shit, you were the new girl, and you were getting all the attention from niggas that used to pay me, so I felt like that money you had was mine. Like I said, I fucked up, though, my bad, you know? But I'm done with it if you're done with it."

I looked over at Prince as he rocked back and forth in the basket, slobbering all over the front of the cart. I was glad that she didn't have the desire to retaliate, though, I didn't want anything to happen to Prince again while I wasn't paying attention. "So, what you doin' out here, Quandra?" I asked as she closed the freezer door. "Let's just say I found a new way to make quick money off thirsty ass niggas," she said, prompting me to walk down the aisle with her. I grabbed my cart and pushed it next to her as she Pinched Prince's cheeks.

"Easy money," she said, "because niggas are so fuckin' stupid, and pussy whipped that they don't even expect it."

"What is it?"

"Look, I don't wanna say too much out here, you know what I'm sayin? I don't know who else is listening to us because it's some nosey muthafuckas out here. That's one thing you find out quick by living out here; it's quiet as fuck and muthafuckas look friendly, but they got they eye on you just waiting to tattle on yo' ass the moment they get the chance."

She made it to the checkout line and placed her items on the register, "Look, I'ma give you my number and shit. Hit me up and we can talk more about it, you know what I'm sayin?" I curiously looked down at the number as she spoke up, "Lyric, I'm not on that bullshit no more. For real. This is all about getting the money together, not working against each other. You wouldn't be competition but at the same time, I get if you don't want to fuck with me. I totally understand," she handed her card to the cashier, "It's your choice but I'm telling you, it's money to be made. As long as you still got that phat ass and a pretty face, you are dangerous as a bitch. Trust me. Niggas haven't prepared for this kind of shit so we in and out, and a bitch like you? Somebody who really ain't scared of shit? It's perfect for you," she reached over and grabbed two candy bars, handing them to the cashier. "Yeah, I heard about yo' ass running with Nas and shit. The whole city knew about yo' ass but that nigga Nas ain't no fuckin' joke, though. I knew he was gon' turn on you sooner or later."

"What are you talking about?"

"Girl," she laughed, "I know why you're here. Yo son right there got kidnapped, Nas wanted him back, and you weren't feeling it, so you vamped. I mean, I still got my ear to the city and shit, you know? Even though we making our rounds through Illinois right now, I still know what's going on in my hometown."

"Makin' y'all rounds?"

"Look, like I said, Lyric, we will discuss all that if you decide to call me. If not, though, it was good seeing you," she took one of the candy bars out of the bag and handed it to Prince, "you still fine and thick as shit, too. If I were a nigga, I'd hit without thinking twice," she said as she laughed, walking away with her bags in her hand. "Hopefully, you'll call me, though. I believe we could use somebody like you, for real."

I looked over at Prince as he put the candy bar in his mouth. I took it from him and unwrapped the paper, breaking a piece off and giving him the rest. I kept my eyes on her as she walked away, switching her ass back and forth, causing her cheeks to shake with each step. I was bored out of my mind since I had been in Rockwall and I knew that the only reason I came here was to lay low and stay out of trouble, but that was becoming tired real quick. I looked down at the number she wrote on a piece of paper, then back towards Prince as he slobbered over the candy bar, making a chocolatey mess. I picked up him out of the shopping cart and left the store, not even picking up what I came in there to get. Quandra had me intrigued, and I was too curious to not at least see what she was talking about.

Chapter 18

Mrs. Butler called me later that night as I was in the hotel room. I told her that I found an apartment and that I was going to move in later this week. She was excited for me and wanted to make plans to come out to visit us. I let her know to come Friday because, in my mind, I had already made the decision to go and see what Quandra was talking about. I knew I wouldn't be able to just sit around for a year without doing anything. I wasn't cut out for that kind of life, and I don't know what made me think that I was.

When Quandra answered the phone, she was happy that I had called. I told her that I would see what they had going on this Friday, and she said it was perfect timing because they were planning something for Saturday night. She said I could get in on it if everything I heard them talk about was cool. Right after we hung up, the unknown number called my phone four times in a row. On the fifth time, I picked it up,

"What, nigga?"

"Bitch, you think I don't know where you at? Huh? You think you are safe?"

"Look, nigga, all you been doin' is sendin' wolf tickets. If you know where I'm at, get me, nigga. You know I'm ready for you or whoever else you got—"

"Aight, bitch. We'll see how ready you are. Yo' ass is gon' end up like that bitch husband. Oh, and by the way, have you heard from Vinny? You might wanna check on that nigga," he laughed, "I'm just saying."

I hung up the phone and called Vinny right away, "What up, Lyric?" I breathed a sigh of relief at the sound of his voice.

"Shit, man. Just out here trying to adjust to this new life. Everything been alright?"

"Yeah, everything been straight. I've just been working and staying low key. I ain't trying to get mixed up in shit out here."

"I feel you. Well, aye, if you need anything just let me know."

"Aight Lyric, but I'm good though. Thanks for hitting me up."

"No doubt. Aye, Vinny... make sure you're careful up there, aight?"

"Aight, no doubt."

"I love you."

"I love you too."

I hung up the phone as a sickening feeling began to stir in my stomach. I didn't know what I would do if something happened to Vinny. That would almost be too much for me to handle and I wanted to tell him to get out of the city, but I didn't want him to worry. Besides that, I knew he wouldn't leave. There was too much of his past in Milwaukee for him to pick up and start somewhere else.

The week flew by and before I knew it, Mrs. Butler was outside the door of my hotel room, "Heeeey, baby! Oh my goodness! Prince!" She hugged me around the neck and then quickly rushed over to Prince as he laughed and reached for her, nearly falling off the bed in the process. I stuck around for a few minutes before I let her know I had to make a run,

"I'll be back in a few, Mom. I have to run and check some things out with the apartment and then I'll be right back."

"Ok, honey, no problem. Be safe, me and Prince will be right here waiting for you to come back."

I headed to the Southside of Rockwall. It looked to be a little more run-down than any other area of the city, and I was surprised to see it myself. I guess every city has its hood, though, no matter how big or small it is. I pulled up to an apartment that had trash and kids' bikes riddled all over the lawn. It was a gated community but the entry and exit gate was broken, so it stayed open for everyone to come and go as they pleased. The swimming pool looked as if you would get some disease from the dirty water as soon as you stepped into it. I called Quandra when I got to the apartment number, and she came out to my car.

"What up, Lyric, I'm glad you here and shit."

"No doubt."

I got out the car and followed her up to the second floor of the apartment complex. I could smell the marijuana smoke as soon as I began walking up the stairs and it completely engulfed me when we walked through the door. Through the thick smoke, I saw lighters firing up more blunts and the silhouettes of various women standing around, watching me as I walked in. "Follow me," Quandra said as we walked through the sea of women straight to the back room. She knocked twice and opened the door. She sat on the bed with a blunt hanging out of her mouth. She blew a cloud of smoke into the air as soon as I walked into the room behind Quandra. Her lips were covered in red, eyebrows arched to perfection. I could see her eyelashes extending out far beyond her eyelids, resembling mosquito legs. Her eyes were sky blue and her peach-colored skin seemed to have been painted onto her body with perfection. On the top of her head, long red hair flowed down like a sensuous fire. She stood up to me as I leaned against the dresser,

"So, you're Lyric, huh?"

"Yeah."

She smiled, "Quandra had told me a lot about you. A lot of good shit," she looked to my side, glancing down at my ass, "Yeah, you thick as a bitch, too."

If I closed my eyes, there was nothing in this world that would have convinced me that she was a white girl. She had the attitude and characteristics of a black woman. She walked over to the window, her ass jiggling effortlessly inside of her gray yoga pants. Just then, two more girls walked in behind me, "Maley, we got one of the niggas down for tomorrow. We workin' on the other two, though." She inhaled another drag of the blunt as she turned around, "Cool. Make sure all five of them niggas are down, otherwise, ain't shit movin." They both turned and left the room as Maley passed the blunt to me. I grabbed it from her hand and inhaled it, allowing the weed to sit in my lungs for a few moments before I blew it back out. I didn't cough once as I passed it back to her. "That was some G shit," she said, smiling in approval of how I just handled the blunt, "not even coughing once? Aight Miss Lyric. Well, like I said, Quandra told me a lot about you, and I think you'd be perfect here, you know what I'm sayin? You got the looks for it and from what I hear, yo' ass is as hard as they come," she leaned towards me, whispering in my ear, "You're the perfect fucking killer."

She winked at me and walked back to her bed, taking another hit of her blunt. I had no idea what the fuck was going on here. I didn't know if this was a prostitution ring or what but it was something about Maley that I liked. It was her assertiveness, the way she seemed to run whatever shit she had going on here. It was in that position of power that I saw for myself. Her pretty smile seemed to get lost in the thick smoke as Quandra leaned on the dresser right beside me. I looked to the right out the window and for a moment, I saw Big Mama's face outlined in the smoke. *That weed must be hitting quick*, I thought to myself as I refocused my eyes in that direction. A tear fell from her eye just as Quandra walked into her, dispersing the vision that I had. She went over to Maley, "So, what you want me to do with her?" she asked as Maley looked right at me. Maley smiled, "Don't do nothing. This is perfect for her, and she doesn't need convincing either, I can tell. She's not going anywhere."

CPSIA information can be obtained
at www.ICGtesting.com
Printed in the USA
LVOW13s0300170417
531053LV00008B/142/P